"If, as I did, you grew up on the likes of *Ultraman, Zatoichi, and Godzilla*, you'll feel right at home with, but also challenged by, the stories in *Where We Go When All We Were is Gone*. It's an exhilarating debut that serves up every guilty-pleasure pop-culture satisfaction one could hope for while simultaneously reframing and refashioning those familiar low-art joys into something singular, unanticipated, and entirely original."
—**Pinckney Benedict, author of** *Town Smokes* **and** *Miracle Boy*

"Ghosts, Godzilla, shape shifters, sea creatures, snow babies; Sequoia Nagamatsu's fantastical characters are nonetheless grounded in modern-day conflicts, creating a fascinating and haunting mix of science and myth, past and present. These are stories of gods and monsters walking among us, told with wit, longing, and wisdom."
—**Timothy Schaffert, author of** *The Swan Gondola,* **an Oprah.com**
   Book of the Week

"These stories deftly breathe new life into the myths and pop culture of an older Japan, bringing them into the modern world and directing them in unexpected ways. It's hard to tell if Nagamatsu holds nothing sacred, or if he holds everything to be. In either case, the effect is the same: these are deft atmospheric romps that a hell of a lot of fun but also worm their way under your skin before you know it. An addictive and compelling debut."
—**Brian Evenson, author of** *Lords of Salem* **(as BK Evenson w/ Rob**
   Zombie) and *A Collapse of Horses*

"Strange, subtle, emotionally resonant–Nagamatsu's fiction is consistently excellent."
—**Kij Johnson, Hugo, Nebula, and World Fantasy Award Winning**
   author of *The Fox Woman, Fudoki,* **and** *At the Mouth of the River of*
   Bees

"The stories in *Where We Go When All We Are is Gone* make up a rich tangle of the familiar and beautifully new. These are bright inventions but they will also satisfy our longing for the stories we have always loved."
—**Ramona Ausubel, author of** *No One is Here Except All of Us* **and** *A*
   Guide to Being Born

Where We Go When All We Were Is Gone

Sequoia Nagamatsu

Black
Lawrence
Press

Black
Lawrence
Press

www.blacklawrence.com

Executive Editor: Diane Goettel
Cover and book design: Amy Freels
Cover image: *Solitary Flight* by Eric Fan, graphite and digital painting

Copyright © Sequoia Nagamatsu 2016
ISBN: 978-1-62557-944-7

All rights reserved. Except for brief quotations in critical articles or reviews, no part of this book may be reproduced in any manner without prior written permission from the publisher: editors@blacklawrencepress.com

Published 2016 by Black Lawrence Press.
Printed in the United States.

The following stories originally appeared in the publications listed:

"The Return to Monsterland" in *Conjunctions*, "Placentophagy" in *Tin House online*, "Rokurokubi" in *Zyzzyva*, "Girl Zero" in *Bat City Review*, "The Peach Boy" in *The Fairy Tale Review*, "The Inn of the Dead's Orientation for Being a Japanese Ghost" in *Puerto Del Sol*, "The Rest of the Way" in *Copper Nickel*, "The Passage of Time in the Abyss" in *Gargoyle*, "Snow Baby" in *Monkeybicycle*, "Where We Go When All We Were Is Gone" in *Green Mountains Review*, "Headwater LLC" in *Lightspeed Magazine,* "Kenta's Posthumous Chrysanthemum" in *The New Delta Review*.

For Cole

This is a dream I dreamed . . .
—Natsume Soseki

I could wish for nothing more than to die for a childish dream in which I truly believed.
—Ryūnosuke Akutagawa

What isn't remembered never happened. Memory is merely a record. You just need to re-write that record.
—Serial Experiments: Lain

Contents

The Return to Monsterland   3

Placentophagy   23

Rokurokubi   29

Girl Zero   43

The Peach Boy   65

The Inn of the Dead's Orientation for Being a
       Japanese Ghost   69

The Passage of Time in the Abyss   95

The Rest of the Way   111

Where We Go When All We Were Is Gone   125

Snow Baby   139

Headwater LLC   143

Kenta's Posthumous Chrysanthemum   157

Transcript:

Woman (Identity Concealed): And we heard a crash outside. People were running down the street. There was smoke. I'm not sure from where. Everywhere? We felt the ground shake, so I grabbed my son and we ran with the crowds. They pushed. We pushed. We didn't dare stop. There was an old woman, and I wanted to help. Everybody was screaming. A man ahead of us turned and pointed up. His eyes wide, his mouth twisted. And that's when I saw it.

Young Boy (Identity Concealed): Godzilla. It was him, I swear. My friends and I were hiding in the school cafeteria with our teachers. He was fighting a giant spider. Picked it up and slammed it right down on a bridge. Bam! Our teachers told us to get away from the windows, but how could we? My friend Toru and I cheered: Go Godzilla Go!

The Return to Monsterland

Train Car, 1998

Mayu called me from the train car that Godzilla had grabbed hold of—no screaming or sobbing, no confessions of great regrets, no final professions of love. She did not ask to speak to our five-year-old daughter, who was unknowingly watching the news coverage of her mother's impending death, as the train crashed into the side of a skyscraper and through a set of power lines. My wife spoke of feeling the radiation of *his* body coursing through her own, the view down *his* cretaceous mouth, an atomic breath swirling in a maelstrom of blue light. And then, before there was nothing but a roar and static, she said: "You should be here; he's simply magnificent."

Godzilla (irradiated Godzillasaurus)

{Descp. Resembles Tyrannosaur with pronounced arms. Dorsal plates similar to Stegosaur. Semi-sapient. Powers: Atomic breath, nuclear pulse, imperviousness to conventional weaponry (and meteor impacts), regenerationw, amphibiousness, telepathy with other Kaiju. Weaknesses: High voltage, Oxygen Destroyer WMD, Anti-Nuclear Energy Bacteria, Cadmium Missiles, MechaGodzilla}

Field Notes: lumber-waddle. posturing roar. rhythmic stomp with son. perhaps a game? picks up palm tree and throws. swats sea gull. Defecates two-meters high—radiation: 15 krad. moves arms up and down. calisthenics or victory dance. long roar. shuffles across beach. throws log into water. throws rock into water.

Two weeks living among their kind on the island reserve we've created for them, and I still can't wrap my head around the love my wife felt for these creatures. During the atomic age, when nations illuminated the atolls dotting the Pacific, we gave birth to many of the Kaiju. Annihilation begetting annihilation when the living ghosts of Hiroshima still roamed the streets. The Ministry of Defense contacted me partly out of kindness, I suspect. The widower of the famous monster biologist, the silent partner who stayed in the lab. I knew the creatures almost as well as Mayu did—the half-life of their blood, the frequency of their telepathic thoughts, the variations of their origins and resurrections. I could, without a doubt, answer Japan's questions of new monsters being born in the wake of Fukushima, of old monsters shaken out of armistice. And so I said yes because I hated their kind, because my daughter, now a college student, still reads the letters her mother left her, because I need to experience the beauty my wife saw before she died.

Dear Ayu,

I had to watch the video of your first steps from the bottom of the ocean. I wish I could have been there. But I guess all of our practice trying to walk paid off! Do you remember how we watched old news broadcasts of the epic Kaiju battles of the 60s? I'd pick you up by the arms, your feet resting on mine, and we'd take one giant step after another, waddling across the living room. Whenever I let you go, there would be a moment where we both thought that you could make that first step on your own. But you flapped your arms like Rodan or Mothra, trying to maintain your balance before crashing to the ground. Your father tells me you're moving non-stop now with your new found freedom, that you circle the house until you're so tired that you need a nap. I wish you were here with me. I hope these letters will help you understand why I was away so much. It's just me, a steel sphere, and two tiny windows right now. Miles of ocean are dead because of us—the Oxygen Destroyer killed a former Godzilla several decades ago along with everything around him: suffocation before the atoms of his body weakened, leaving nothing but bone. A shark hunts in vain—still. A jelly billows past like a cloud. I rake away layers of shells and fish husks from his skeleton with the submarine's robotic arm, collect him piece-by-piece. Godzilla died then because we didn't understand, because we are always afraid—and despite him saving us from danger time and again, we never seem to learn.

Mu

Sunken civilization. Geologic curiosity. Aquatic paradise. Scuba dive excursion. Mu, home of the Nacaal, shaken beneath the waves overnight—temples entombed in lava, megalith highways to the Mariana Trench. The Nacaal, catamaran refugees, ancestors of Egypt and the Fertile Crescent. Manda, water dragon guardian, still defending the Nacaal after millennia. At a college dive, Mayu and I discussed her dissertation on the Kaiju as Heritage, creatures who came before us, were created by us, that served us. Creatures, I added, that no longer belonged. But we must find a way for them to belong, she insisted. "Try reasoning with a three-story lizard," I said. "Tell that to the parents of children who died when these creatures decided to throw down on their school." A piece of Mu has been placed off the coast of the reserve for Manda to protect, a collection of pillars, the worn smirk of a sandstone warrior, three-thousand pounds of drowned mountain. Five miles of ocean surrounded by an electromagnetic field. This is what we can give them. This is where they belong.

Mothra (Moth Goddess, current stage: larval)

{Descp. Segmented Brown body. Blue eyes. Pronounced mandibles. Powers: Silken spray. Several beam weapons. Strong psychic communication. As an adult, able to create gale force wind with wings. Lightning from antennae. Effectively immortal (phoenix lifecycle). Travels with faery sisters, the Elias—three inch women in red tunics.}

Field Notes: Undulates around island. tries to follow butterflies and moths. visits other Kaiju. sways head with Varan. chews on shrubs and grasses. draws mandalas on beach with body. sends sonic pulse to Manda. The Elias, Lora and Moll, ride its back. The Elias laugh frequently. whispers. song.

A glorified grub, a far cry from the bright orange and yellow wings that Mayu and my daughter loved. Perhaps the most beloved of the Kaiju because she is a Goddess, because through her spritely companions, we understand the moth's chirps, the roars and groans of other Kaiju. "Godzilla doesn't hate humans but humans hate us," the little sisters declared on national television. Fair enough, I say. But he still flattened my favorite soba shop in the country with several elderly ladies inside, used Tokyo Tower like a toothpick.

Maybe we shouldn't have used missiles, maybe we could have spent time coming to an understanding. But parlays are an afterthought when people are running out of their cars and screaming down the street. Mayu said that's typical human behavior, the kind of trait that would ruin humanity in the end: shoot first, ask questions later. She reminded me it was the Kaiju who saved us from alien invasions—the Kilaakians, the Millenians. Ayu, who became quite the activist in her junior high class, following her mother's letters as text, would always say, "Kaiju don't kill people; people kill people" and "Love is the greatest weapon of all!"

The Elias sisters pay me no mind most of the time but occasionally flutter around my head, giggling like school girls, providing me insight into each of the creatures: *Godzilla is very sad today. Godzilla remembers your wife and is sorry. Godzilla cannot help being Godzilla. Manda is lonely. There were once many sea dragons in the sea. Manda knows Mu is far away. Mothra remembers when humans were not here. Mothra says those were peaceful times. Mothra says quiet will come again one day. Baragon has indigestion from eating a strange plant. Gorosaurus wants to find love. Angurius wants to get to know Rodan better. Nobody really likes Kumonga. Kumonga is grumpy. Kumonga will try to kill you.*

Dear Ayu,

Yesterday I brought you with me to the NHK television studio to talk to the Elias. You've just turned two now, so I imagine you won't remember any of this except for impressions of faery feet dancing on your tummy, making you laugh, of Lora and Moll singing lost melodies into your ear. Atlantean ballads, Babylonian hymns, they said. You held your Mothra stuffed animal, your most prized possession, that has watched over you in your crib since you were born. Lora and Moll reclined on the plush wings, as I interviewed them. I have to admit, I'd like to fancy myself the Margaret Mead of the Kaiju world. The people have stopped running, little one. At least for now. The time has come to listen to those we call monsters.

The sisters talked of Mothra being part of a menagerie of Earth deities, each with a counterpart, creating balance in the world. The Earth created Battra to destroy evil but this moth became evil itself. And so Mothra was created to bring good into the world. When darkness rises, the forces of good must restore balance. One cannot exist without the other you see (even for the creatures humanity creates). And so some of our monsters are reborn when we need them. I try explaining this idea of balance to you during our hikes. You on my back, as I shed calories at the base of Mt. Fuji. I tell you these things in the hope that you'll grow to appreciate life, to see humanity in concert with the Earth instead of in control of it. Your father and I, despite what he might believe about his semi-annual donations to environmental non-profits, disagree in this matter.

Back home, I put you on the quilt your grandmother made you with your Play Zone console while I transcribed my interview with the Elias. I reclined on your father's chair and concentrated on my work. You've figured out how to play Pop Goes the Weasel by pressing a red button and seem genuinely delighted every time you hear the music play, as if it's a new discovery. I put on my headphones and ignored you for the rest of the afternoon. I gave you a sippy cup and read through a study of a colleague's pharmaceutical research based on the DNA of sixteen captive shape shifters. Imagine, anti-aging skin! You stared at me blankly. You did not cry or fuss. You've always been good about letting mommy be.

Angurius (Irradiated Ankylosaurus w/ Styracosaurian cranial features)

{Descp. Long, clubbed spiked tail. Orange spikes and horns on gray skin. Five brains (one in head, others near limbs—heightened reflexes & locomotion). Capable of bi-pedal motion but generally quadruped. Powers: Lacking in ranged attacks and special abilities but rarely concedes in battle. Advanced burrowing abilities. Use of spiked carapace by jumping backwards onto enemies. Able to curl into ball and travel at high speed. Oldest and perhaps most consistent ally of Godzilla.}

Field Notes: Chews on palm. Burrows past Kumonga. Emerges beside Godzilla. Rolls between hills. Rolls into coconuts. Perhaps bocce? Rests on carapace. Godzilla spins friend. Both roar. Both wave arms. Follows Godzilla. Sleeps with Godzilla.

Late for our dinner and distracted by work, Mayu said yes to my marriage proposal almost as an afterthought. I honestly didn't care. I was the safe bet for her, the guy who would always be there (and I always was even when she was nowhere to be found). Maybe I thought marrying my best friend and colleague would be enough and the rest would take care of itself. She could grow to love me— and our professional differences would stoke the passion that I thought we had found in our night long debates in graduate school when we would seamlessly shift from biochemistry to the bedroom. "You're like a puppy barking at the television," she'd say. "You're adorably confused about the reality of things." And I'd say, "You're the hippie that's doing all the barking." She was a ten to my marginal six (in both beauty and professional pedigree), something my jackass friends would often remind me of, and perhaps it was this fact that, in part, fed a nagging insecurity, prompting me to do nothing when I suspected Mayu was having an affair with her research assistant—a blond post-doc from Berkeley who looked more surfer than scientist. As long as she came home to me. As long as we were still a family.

Angurius is not the strongest of the Kaiju. He does not fly, does not shoot lasers from his horns or mouth. But he is loyal to his allies. He never gives up even when he is beaten down. Ruled by atomic instinct and rage, even these creatures understand friendship, something that I've read about in papers but could never believe until I lived among them. And I wonder even after all of their deaths and rebirths if they remember—or is who they are and what they mean to each other not so much memory as stitching in the fabric of their being?

Dear Ayu,

I really wanted to take you with me during the filming of my National Geographic special but your father said the journey would be too arduous for a little girl who already has a full plate with kindergarten and after school English classes. He worries too much. (And could you think of a better education than this?) You would absolutely love it. Maybe he would just miss you. I know you hear us fighting sometimes, and I want you to know it's not your fault. Mommy has to be away a lot, so sometimes daddy gets lonely. He gets jealous because you want to be with me instead of him even though I can't be there for you every day when you get home from school. I can't take you to do fun things on the weekend like going to Ueno Zoo to look at the Red Pandas ... but know that I really want to. Be a good girl for him. He does try, and he loves you. One day I'll be home more. You'll come home after school and you can tell me about your friends, show

me a project you're proud of—macaroni necklaces, cardboard diora-
mas, book reports dotted with stickers from your teacher. But there
is still so much work to be done. Oh, the things you're missing right
now. My research assistant, Tyler, who you've met (I believe you said
he looked like "in the movies"), scouted out locations for us to film:
abandoned parts of Tokyo, Paris, London, and Cairo that were once
battlegrounds of great Kaiju battles. We traveled to Monsterland to
talk to scientists doing experiments on containing the Kaiju with
chemical mists and electromagnetic fields. Containment vs. exter-
mination is our goal, so we can foster better relationships with these
terribly misunderstood creatures. Your father sent me photos of you
and your grandmother under a cherry blossom tree. Are those new
overalls? I've only been away three months and yet you seem to have
grown so much. Enclosed are photos of me and Tyler with some of the
Kaiju in the background.

Rodan (Irradiated Pteranodon)

{Descp. 200 meter wingspan. Reddish-brown. Powers: Immune to atomic breath and gravity beams. Shockwaves while flying. High winds via wings. Quite strong despite spindly appearance. History of self-sacrifice to help others.}

Field Notes: crushes rocks with beak. spreads wings. blows down
trees. topples Kumonga. takes off. circles island. perches on mountain
top. extended screech.

My father worked long hours at the post office for decades to provide for me and my siblings. He took us fishing on the weekends and gave

us what little money he had to buy manga—Ultraman, Space Pirate
Captain Harlock. His only joy was watching baseball on television
while drinking a cold Sapporo. My mother dreamed of becoming
a nightclub singer (and from what I understand had interest from
a Russian owned Roppongi club), but I would only ever know her
voice from the lullabies she sang in my childhood. I never expected
Mayu and I to follow in my parent's footsteps, giving ourselves so
completely to our children. Our livelihoods, particularly Mayu's,
required a certain level of commitment. But I did expect some sacrifice, some change in her that never happened. I never minded
being the one to chauffeur Ayu, cook meals, help with homework,
and read bedtime stories. But, if I'm honest, Ayu grew up only with
the mystique of her mother, the legend of her spun from letters and
occasional visits. Tell her I love her, Mayu would say whenever I was
on the phone with her. Give her this for me. Send me pictures. Mayu
became the giver of gifts, the adventurer with stories, the person my
daughter turned to for understanding when I became the target of
hatred. After Rodan transferred his life force to Godzilla so that he
could defeat MechaGodzilla, Mayu talked on American television
about the love of Godzilla for his son in defeating his enemy, about
the sacrifice of Rodan in helping his friend to victory. "These creatures," she said. "Are more like us than we'd like to admit. They love
and they protect that which they love. They may fight sometimes,
yes. But, when the cards are down, they would do anything for each
other."

Dear Ayu,

I hope you and your father have fun this weekend at Disneyland. I can't express how sorry I am that I had to leave at the last minute. I know I'm not there for you as much as I should be. I keep saying this, I know. And I hope all I'm doing now will be somehow worth it. I've written almost two-hundred letters to you. Some of them are written to you as you are now, my innocent, silly girl. But much of what I write is for myself and for a much older version of you, a you that has fallen in love, chased a dream, gotten your heart broken, learned lessons the hard way, found a soul mate when you weren't looking for one, and perhaps even entered the strange world of motherhood (something I know I can't fully claim to know a lot about). The last time I went to Disneyland was the weekend after your father proposed. We rode every ride at least twice, but we spent most of the day just walking, observing the families that we might one day resemble. I asked your father, "Is that what you want for us?" And he said he wanted that life very much. I told him I did, too. And maybe it wasn't exactly the truth, but I said it anyway because I wanted to believe children and pets and a mortgage would make everything easier by oddly making my life fuller. Anyway . . . I enjoyed your phone call yesterday. I'm glad you and your friend Haruka made up on the playground even after she pushed over your block tower. Sometimes friends do messed up things even if they care about you. But it's important to try to work things out, to forgive if at all possible. The world's a big, scary place, little one. Company is always nice. Ride all the rides, even the scary ones. Take pictures. And tell your daddy that mommy says you can have a treat in the gift shop.

Birth Island

Deserted island. Respite from the world. Godzilla and Zilla Junior quality time after brushes with death. Birth island where the king of the monsters found fatherhood. Birth island where the children of monsters are allowed to play.

Conception following an ultimatum wasn't the ideal. Now or never, I told Mayu. Yes, I'm unhappy I said. How long can we really wait? In retrospect we were both being unfair. Me because I was telling my wife who may never have been in love with me to have a child in order to save our domestic best-friendship. Her because she, for whatever reason, could never admit the truth about how she felt. We gave permission to each other to get comfortable with our discomfort. At the hospital, after she had given birth, Mayu said: "I don't know how to be a mother." I told her no one does at first. She looked down at Ayu, nestled in her arms and looked back up at me, "What if I never feel like I'm her mother?"

1999: Mommy, I had a dream that…

2000: Dear Mommy, Daddy won't let me….

2001: Dear Mommy, the kids at school…

2002: Dear Mommy, I miss you. I hate the monsters that took you away.

2005: Dear Mom, I'm organizing a presentation with my friends about protecting the Kaiju. I've already collected signatures of almost everybody in my school to send to the Prime Minister.

2008: Dear Mom, I've started seeing a boy, but I don't think I like, like him. I got perfect scores again in all my science classes. Let's not talk about gym class.

2012: Dear Mom, great news! I've been accepted to Osaka University! Your old assistant, Tyler, is a visiting professor there. He took me to lunch. He said he was excited that I was admitted. He said you were a remarkable woman and that he was sorry the world lost you so early.

Minilla (Infant Godzillasaurus)

{Descp. Smaller version of his father without pronounced armored plates. Generally fearful of other monsters. Playful in nature. Powers: radioactive smoke rings, telepathy with father, ability to shrink to human size w/some human vocal abilities. Some history of convincing father to be gentler with humankind}

Field Notes: runs circles around father. shrinks in size and plays in small cave. tumble rolls. waves arm at me. hello? twirls. tiny roar. endearing roar. throws coconut at father.

Every year until there was nothing left (Ayu had just turned fourteen), the two of us would take a small packet of her mother's ashes and scatter them at a site of a Kaiju incident. We traveled to three continents, eleven countries, and four islands. For the last year, we stopped by Ueno station in Tokyo, walked upstairs to where we could overlook the train tracks that were lifted off the ground by Godzilla nine years prior. Ayu had grown from silence to hatred of all things non-human to a champion for those creatures who needed a voice. I was proud of the young woman she was becoming. I'm proud of the woman she has become. I emptied the last of her mother into her palms and she held them over the walkway, her fingers still curled shut. "Goodbye, mom," she said. "I won't stop writing." She opened her hands and let the draft of a passing train carry away the ashes.

Dear Ayu,

I'll be taking the next train to Tokyo tomorrow, one of only a handful being let in for research and military personnel while Godzilla paces downtown. Your father tells me the two of you are doing quite well with grandma and grandpa in Nara. Like camping, he says—you in your Hello Kitty pup tent in the living room. Hopefully your school will reschedule your play after all this is over. I was very much looking forward to seeing you as a dancing sunflower. Your father also tells me that he practically had to drag you out of the city because you wanted to stay and see Godzilla, study him like me. My sweet, little scientist. Maybe one day you'll be able to join me. It's been many years since any Kaiju have surfaced like this (especially without any obvious nuclear incidents on our part), so we're very interested in finding out why Godzilla has suddenly returned, why he is upset.

Your father and I were on the phone for hours last night. I said little. I stared at the picture of you and me that was taken after we took you home from the hospital. Our street was blanketed in Cherry Blossom petals. You are crying. I look like I'm going to cry, and I remember being incredibly sad. I had lost a part of myself when I brought you into the world. The idea of being a mother, of you felt so much more complete and less alien when you were still inside me. Maybe I've been running away ever since, so I could keep this fantasy, these idealized visions of your father and I teaching you how to ride a bike, going on picnics, laughing over some stupid joke over dinner. But perhaps it's time to run back.

Kumonga (Irradiated Arachnid)

{Descp. Brown. Two-stories tall. Slender, prehensile appendages. Serrated legs. Powers: thick webbing, stinger, appendages used for impaling, cutting, and holding. Jumping abilities.}

Field Notes: mummifies wild boar in silk. repairs webbing between hillside. shoots silk spray at passing seagulls. circles territory of other Kaiju.

Kumonga senses the vibrations of my footsteps, follows me with bejeweled eyes. Unlike some of the other Kaiju, Kumonga has not shown higher intelligence, a propensity for sacrifice and friendship. His world is one of binaries: moving vs. non-moving, alive vs. dead, light vs. dark, cold vs. hot. He straddles a ridge, watching over a valley. He could jump, impaling me with one of his legs as he lands. He could shoot silk and draw me close to his fangs, injecting my body with digestive juices as he wraps me for a later meal. Through my binoculars, I can see the tiny hairs of his abdomen, the reflection of the valley several times over in his eyes. That there are several emergency hatches to the island's underground lab near Kumonga's territory is no coincidence. In the wild and in households, spiders keep insect populations low. Their venom, sometimes deadly and painful, can be engineered to treat pain, relax muscles. But Kumonga's venom is uranium rich. His insects are humans and large animals. His appetite too savage for a tiny, blue world.

Kumonga raises his body, spreads his front limbs wide, revealing his reach. I open a hatch as his limbs coil in for a jump. Beneath ground, I hear the pitter patter of his legs, the chittering of his mandibles. A three by three titanium square and twenty meters of soil and rock separate us. And I can't help but remember news footage of the pounding of children in a school bus turned on its side as Kumonga approached, the seismic readings Mayu took of his legs rapping on the ground, calling for a mate the nuclear age failed to provide.

"And you still think they belong?" I asked Mayu.
"Do we even belong anymore?"
"The destruction they cause..."
"The destruction we cause. Don't you see beauty in them?"
"There are many beautiful things in nature that are best kept hidden."

Dear Ayu,

I hope your first year at university has been going well. I'm very proud of you. When your mother was alive, you wanted to follow her to the ends of the Earth. You have her letters and her phone calls and the handful of memories of days you spent together. This is who the woman I called my wife was to you. She is the woman who chased monsters, protected them from the ugliness of humanity. She was other things certainly, to me, to those she worked with, to people in our family. You remember us fighting and me being the bad guy some-times. You stood perfectly still as I cried onto your tiny shoulders, squeezing you tightly after static was all that remained of my last conversation with a woman who I loved and hated and respected. Her last words: "You should be here; he's simply magnificent." And I think I'm coming close to being able to see what she saw, but I need your help. I need you because you're the best parts of her, the parts that flourished in the imaginings of your memory, in the wonder of people who watched her television shows and read her books.

Enclosed are tickets and travel arrangements for your school break. In many ways, this will be your return to Monsterland, as you've been here in your dreams, in your drawings and the models you've built where the Kaiju live happily with Barbies and Totoro. There is no question the Kaiju will get loose again. New Kaiju will be born by design and accident. They will defend us and they will attack us. And they'll die only to be reborn, eventually returning to the haven we've created for them. We can run tests, observe their behavior to forecast the probabilities of these things. But I'd like to believe that your mother is here, too, that she's become part of this cycle. We haven't always seen eye-to-eye, but I need you to help me past the primeval roars and stomps, the image of a train car hanging from claws. I need help seeing the beauty of a radioactive glow within an embryo that can breathe life into the ancient, transform the ordinary into the incredible, make chaos somehow make sense.

Summer Recipe:

Placenta Bloody Mary

- ½ cup diced human placenta
- 2oz vodka
- 3½ oz tomato juice
- Dollop tobacco sauce
- Dash horseradish
- Smidgen Worcestershire sauce
- Pinch salt & pepper
- Sprinkle chili powder
- 3 to 4 placenta strips (half inch thick)
- Lime wedge

*Blend everything except placenta strips and lime wedge. Use strips and wedge as garnish

Placentophagy

My doctor always asked how I would prepare it, the placenta. Powdered and encapsulated for my Yuki—two, three, four or more a day depending on my level of sadness and how much I believed the vitamins and hormones within the tissue would make me whole again. Pan fried and stuffed into dumplings for Toru. A smoothie and two yakitori for Keiko. But my doctor remains silent this morning, collapses into the deepest bow, and offers the plastic container as I get situated in a wheelchair. Somewhere in the building Ayu's tiny body, caught in the strained expression of her first and last cry, rests in drawer, waiting for someone to fetch her.

When we get home from the hospital, I put the placenta in the freezer. Recipes and tips for preparation cover the fridge. The children, young as they are, know enough to keep their distance, to remain silent, and move slowly through the house like ghosts. I hear their footsteps outside my door. I hear my husband whispering to them. In bed, I flip through a legal pad covered with notes about ancient Chinese methods for dehydrating the placenta—*Zi He Che*—(steamed with ginger to shrink the organ before heating in the stove), variations of herbal blends for tea. My husband has created a fort of pillows and blankets around me. He says:
"We don't have to do it this time—just because we have it."

"We should do it because we have it," I say. I write down daal and naan. I write cumin and cardamom. But I'm not sure if I want to do Indian. "I need to do something."

Despite being regarded as unusual, eating the placenta (placentophagy), can help women restore hormonal balance after labor and provide much needed vitamins and nutrients: Iron, B6, B12, Estrogen, Progesterone. Before I had Yuki, I was determined to do everything possible to ensure that I would be okay, that motherhood would not leave me. Most mammals in the animal kingdom eat their placenta to solidify the bond with their offspring, to ease pain, and encourage lactation. Ingesting what has given life to connect to life and ensure survival. I once watched documentary of a lioness lap at her placenta, licking it clean of blood before consuming it in a couple of bites. I admired the instinct, envied it.

The Baganda of Uganda believe the placenta is a spirit double and plant the organ beneath a fruit tree. When the fruit is ripe, the family has a big feast after which the parents make love, delivering the copy of their child's spirit into the mother. In Iceland, the placenta is called *fylgia*, which means guardian angel. Placed beneath the floor of the mother's bed, the guardian angel would be protected and grow into an ox, a bear, a wolf, or whatever guide best suited a child. These traditions brought me comfort with my other children. But I am not a lioness. We do not have a yard or a tree to plant (and I cannot wait). And if there was a guardian angel somewhere inside the purple membrane inside our freezer, a cub, a wolf pup, an eaglet, she failed to do her job.

Later, in the kitchen, my husband stands behind me as I slice my placenta into jerky-like strips, running my fingers over the thick tangle of veins that streamed life to my daughter for the past several months. I do not know what I am going to make, but I turn around and ask my husband to get the olive oil, as I take down our largest frying pan and turn on the stove.

I pick up a piece of placenta and instead of placing it on the pan, I hold it in my hand for a while, its cold, jellyfish-like consistency between my fingers—a leech, a sea slug, the flat worms my oldest said he dissected in school that could duplicate themselves if you cut them. I pour a glass of Beaujolais Nouveau for myself and my husband and, realizing what I need to do, pop a slice in my mouth, barely chewing, letting it slide down my throat. My husband stares at me, his mouth agape. I grab two more slices and give him one. He examines it, sniffs it. I hold his free hand and tell him, "On three."

And we swallow.

And we sit across from each other at our dining table with the tray of placenta between us. And we will stay there until everything that connected me to my daughter, all that allowed her to be for the span of a breath, is taken back from the world and absorbed inside us.

Support Group for Humans w/ Demonic Afflictions
Every First Tuesday in Yoyogi Park @ Midnight

- Help your human partner cope
- Learning to control your abilities
- Make-up Tutorial: Masking your Monster
- Legal Advice
- Game Nights
- Singles Mixers
- Your Powers in the Bedroom

Yokai Underground Quarterly

Rokurokubi

I scarcely recognize my childhood friend Aki anymore. It's not so much the sexual reassignment surgery, although it was strange at first to call him by her new name, Ayaka, but the cosmetic follow-ups designed to make her look like Nicole Kidman.

Apart from the drugs and riding-crop scene, I admire what she has with Luka. They've both been together longer than my wife, Sayuri, and I, first meeting at the Fuji Rock Festival eight years ago, but have managed to keep that first-date excitement alive. They're good people and the only ones who know about my secret: at night I can stretch my neck.

At first, I figured it was part of puberty and the rest of my body would catch up. But when I awoke in the middle of one night with my nose pressed up against the ceiling, it became apparent something else was going on.

Now I loom over their cluttered apartment in Sapporo with a webcam in my mouth, filming Ayaka riding Luka hard with her newfound womanhood.

I stretch my neck a few meters longer and circle the room for a final shot, zooming in on Ayaka as her body undulates like a dying fish. Then I let the webcam fall on a pillow.

Luka pours a glass of whiskey and tips it to my lips. The warmth crawls down to my body, lying in bed kilometers away. There's something very close to childhood about not having the rest of your body around—the helplessness of not having your arms, the emasculated aspect of your genitals being half way across the city.

Ayaka spoon feeds me some cold Chicken Tika Masala and leans into Luka for a massage. She arches her back, still marveling at the work of a Dr. Lam Poh Min. "Have you talked with your wife yet?" Ayaka asks, as she starts burning crystal.

I shake my head, "You mean about this?" I coil over myself and eyeball my neck, "Or her affair?"

"I guess both."

"No, I don't know how to start that conversation. She's barely around for any kind of talking."

"Just get it out in the open, man. You can't fix this shit hiding," Luka says.

My meth addict friends have a point. When Ayaka has two syringes ready to go, she taps my head. I watch over them, making sure they're all right, monitoring their breathing as they give into the rush. Even like this, they look good together. I stretch my neck back home after they've fallen asleep, squeezing my head into the toilet, and make my way to suburbia, using the pipes beneath the city streets as my own personal metro.

Back home the next morning, I scrub my neck free of grime and cover any scrapes with anti-bacterial cream and makeup. My wife's yelling to me from outside my bedroom door. We keep separate bedrooms on account of my snoring, which, in reality, has just been a long-term hoax to keep my secret hidden. "I might take the nightshift again. The department store is sending someone to take back the sofa in the evening," she says. I grunt and hear her creaking on the cheap hardwood laminate she insisted on buying. "Did you hear me? Night shift. Sofa pick-up. I've decided it's too expensive," she says louder.

I eat my breakfast—sausage links and perfectly fried eggs with the yolk still intact. If it weren't for the George Foreman Grill I bought in America when I was getting my wasted masters in literature, I'd probably starve.

Sayuri walks down the stairs with a garment bag slung over a shoulder. Her hair has been sculpted with the patience of a bonsai practitioner but then deliberately tousled to look like she doesn't give a damn. If I ask what's inside the garment bag, she'll say it's a kimono just in case the front desk is slow and the restaurant needs extra help. And while this is a credible excuse, I'm also not blind. I've seen enough romance movies and daytime dramas to know the signs. When I find a receipt that shouldn't exist, when I can't take it anymore, I confront her with inconsequential questions and remarks. Part of me wants to save this marriage.

"Why don't we just keep the sofa," I say. "We're never going to have anything nice if we keep returning things."

"What do you mean?" asks Sayuri. She assumes that high school bitch pose where her hip is shifted to one side. "You're the one that's always telling me to watch the money." She dismisses me with an open palm and opens the front door. "Do whatever you want."

While my ability continued to manifest itself as I grew up, I thought I could get away with anything. I'd walk home from school gazing down alleyways, at the life between the cracks of gentle society—the junkies crouched by trash bags, the biker gangs flaunting the horsepower between their legs to prostitutes on smoke breaks. At night, I stretched my neck to visit these people. I tried to be discreet. Of course, being a teenager, coupled with Aki daring me to steal women's underwear, I sometimes put myself at risk of exposure. Aki, armed with a walkie-talkie, would plant himself outside our target's house and direct me to windows or other points of entry. I'd stay as low to the ground as possible, stretching my neck through storm drains and bushes during the journey.

"Water Lily 1 to Red Leader," Aki would say, as he peered through his grandfather's binoculars before giving me the green light. "Target has undressed and is in the shower."

"Red team is go," I'd respond through my headset. We undertook these operations nearly every night. Our homeroom teacher wore baby blue thongs. The senior girl who tutored me in geometry wore cotton ones that said "This side up" on the backside. I feared I would get caught, sent away to some government facility to be prodded and dissected. But who would believe reports of a head with an infinite neck, zipping through city streets with lingerie hanging from its teeth?

One evening during my university years, after spying on businessmen paying escorts to dress like anime characters, I came upon something unexpected. Or rather, it came upon me. From the shadows of a nearby park where homeless people sleep in summer, and monumental ice sculptures are carved in winter, the head of a bearded, old man emerged. He had no body to speak of and no elongated neck. Just the head, floating about like a tiny dirigible of flesh and bone. He introduced himself as Ken, a Nukekubi—a man whose head could detach from its body at night, and referred to me as a Rokurokubi—a long neck.

"People have called our kind demons for centuries," Ken said, as he made careful circles around my neck, a trail of blue light following his head like the tail of a comet. "You shouldn't be so careless when you're out at night." I assured Ken that I took precautions to avoid being seen, but he was a member of the war generation who believed young people knew little or nothing. "The neck of a Rokurokubi must return to its normal size by dawn or will remain elongated until the following day," he continued. Ken explained that during the war, he had met another like myself who had lost track of time, spying on the enemy. At daybreak, Chinese soldiers clearly saw what was human flesh, hiding within the rice paddies, and opened fire, tearing away at the Rokurokubi's neck until it severed entirely. I told Ken that I got the picture and thanked him for the advice. He examined me, narrowing his eyes, and shot off into the darkness, emanating a horrific shrieking sound, a luminescent mist left in his wake like a trail of miniature stars. I never saw him again.

When Sayuri and I first met at a café after talking online for several months, I knew it would be difficult keeping my secret. But we had already shared so much between the expressive *(^_~)* emoticons and the I <3 U's before we signed off every night. We cradled our cappuccinos with one hand and played with each other's fingers like amorous spiders with the other. Then she told me she had something to confess.

"Do you remember how I told you I came close to getting married once?" She began. "Well, there's a reason why it didn't work out. Another reason." She took both my hands.

"It doesn't matter," I said.

She closed her eyes and leaned across the table. "I'm Buraku," she muttered under her breath. She said it so fast that I could barely be certain if I heard her correctly. But then she said it again, "I'm Buraku. My family moved to Hokkaido after the war to start fresh. We had hoped records of our lineage were destroyed in the air raids."

"But your fiancé's family found out. I can't believe people still believe in that caste shit." She bit her lower lip and her eyes became glazed like a pair of polished stones. I took her head in my hands, covering both her ears, and kissed her for the first time.

I had planned to tell Sayuri before we got married, after all, she had opened herself so much to me that I felt I could trust her with anything. But in the crevices of all the locked doors, all the excuses I told Sayuri when I stretched my neck, a tension had grown between us. I needed to wait for the perfect moment. I needed to be absolutely sure she'd stay. When the recession hit, I lost my lectureship at Hokkaido University and took the first job I could get. She deserved more than a door-to-door salesman selling solar water heaters. She's the only thing I've ever really wanted in my life, and I was afraid she'd leave. Any courage I amassed to tell Sayuri the truth had vanished. And now, five years later, I have the same fears because I never told her, because I couldn't give her children and because of her assumptions, whatever they might be.

I slowly get ready for work, hoping to resolve the morning's argument with Sayuri before I have to leave. I call her but there's no answer. So far this month, I haven't sold a single solar water heater. I spend the day on trains scoping out residential neighborhoods. In the late afternoon, high school girls with short, plaid skirts pile on. I try not to look, but there's just too many of them. I tuck my chin into my chest and pretend to sleep. Today, I've already knocked on over fifty doors. Most are a mixture of senior couples and lonely housewives, and, lately, I've been fantasizing about sleeping with the latter. I guess like any guy, the thought's always there. Do I really want to get back at Sayuri? I don't know, part of me does, although this whole mess is partly my fault. I'm not sure she would even care. But I want her to care. I want jealousy to eat her up inside. At least then, I'd know a small part of her still loved me. It would give me hope that we can somehow get through this.

When I get home, Sayuri isn't there, so I decide to go to Ayaka and Luka's. I need to talk to someone. If anything, they'll have something to help me forget about my life for a few hours. When I pop out of the toilet, Poison's "Talk Dirty to Me" is belting out of the iPod dock—a classic of the hair band era if ever there was one. Luka throws a towel over my head and pats me dry, making sure to get any toilet water out of my ears. He passes me a joint and holds it for me as I inhale while Ayaka, probably already on something, can't seem to stop petting me. The time goes by fast. At first, I talk about my marriage—How I've driven Sayuri away with my secret, if my urge to spy on people is a demonic quirk or just some addiction, but soon I lose focus, and as my eyes become heavier, we move onto other topics: a full back tattoo Luka wants done of a Bengal Tiger, if it would be possible to light an entire house with fireflies. I'm crashing and can barely keep my eyes open. Ayaka tells me she can wake me up in a few hours if I want to sleep, and then flinches at a Tyrannosaurus Rex on the TV. I can hear Ken's voice warning me that my neck will remain elongated for a full day if I don't return to my body before dawn. I'm not sure if I can trust Ayaka like this. I retract my neck and drift off.

I spend the day in bed, the sheets damp and soiled with sewer debris from my journey home. When I wake up in the evening, I order a large hand tossed—half Hawaiian Delight and half Tuscan Chicken and heat up a bottle of Sake while I wait for Sayuri to return. I save the Hawaiian side for her but end up eating it myself. I have a stack of evidence I've collected over the year—restaurant receipts and pay stubs from the hotel that proves she doesn't work when she claims. I suppose I could have always followed her, but I didn't want to be "that guy". I can't decide whether to burn it all or shove it in her face. I imagine us making up, saying we're sorry and having a go on the kitchen counter, but I also see us arguing, and I come awfully close to slapping her with the backside of my hand. This last thought frightens me, and I decide to take a shower to clear my head. I don't hear Sayuri coming in under the noise of the water but hear her footsteps as I step out of the tub. I cinch a towel around my waist. She's walking back and forth in the living room with a stupid grin, text messaging someone. The phone vibrates a moment later. She laughs. Beads of water are running down my body, and there's a puddle at my feet. She puts her phone away when she sees me standing in the hall.

"I was going to save you some pizza but when you didn't come back—"

"I ate at work. We were really busy today. A bunch of Russians are in town for some convention," she explains. "Could you dry off? You're going to ruin the floor."

"It's not real wood," I say. "Did you get my messages?"

"No, my cell was stashed in my work locker." She glances at the clock above the dinner table.

"Who was that on the phone?" I ask, and I realize this is it. This is when we're going to throw everything out there. Sayuri looks annoyed, but there's also sadness in her eyes. It's dead night, and I can feel my neck wanting to stretch. But Sayuri would probably run out, screaming if I did it now. No, I need to work up to that—one problem at a time.

"It was the hotel. They need help tonight," she says. "I have to leave again soon." And with that, I grab the pile of receipts I have stashed on top of the china cabinet and throw them in front of her. They flutter in the air for a moment and come to rest at her feet. She stares at the papers and looks up slowly. "So, what do you want to hear?" She makes her way past me, and heads toward the master bedroom. I follow, pulling on her arm. I have to stop myself from stretching my neck and lunging my head out in front of her like a Jack-in-the-Box. I stand in the doorway, watching her undress and go through our closets. She tosses a black skirt on the bed, one I've never seen before.

"Just say it." I raise my voice more than I intended.

"What? That I'm fucking my manager?" She says this with her eyes wrinkled, as if to hurt me even more. But her face quickly softens, and she takes a few steps toward me. Okay, I've heard her say it, and now I don't know what the hell to do. I don't want to yell at her or hit her. But I don't want to leave either. I stand there, sinking against the wall. "I'm sorry," she whispers. "I didn't mean it to come out like that. But this wasn't just me. You know that."

"I nod my head. Sayuri takes my damp cheeks in both of her hands and kisses my brow. Part of me wants to ask questions—How many times? Is he better than me? Does she love him? Another part wants to stretch my neck and wrap around her body like a vine and finally tell her, "Look! Look! It's not my fault. I'm a freak. I thought you wouldn't understand." But I don't say anything.

"I'll be home tomorrow for a little while to take a nap. But I work at night. That's the truth. We can talk over dinner the day after if you want," she says, and then walks down the hall and out the front door.

I don't go to Ayaka or Luka's place nor do I stalk strangers as usual. I need to be alone. I want to be as far away from here as possible. I stretch my neck out the bedroom window and swing up to the sky until the tops of skyscrapers become minuscule dots and the congested expressways look like Christmas lights. The occasional migratory bird crosses my path, no doubt perplexed by my presence. I go higher still, and it becomes difficult to breathe. The air has gotten fiercely cold, and the condensation below my nostrils is beginning to freeze. I stop to look at the blanket of clouds below, at the unobstructed stars above. I've never known a quiet like this. If I could only bring Sayuri up here then she'd understand. I play the evening over in my mind. After a lifetime of observing people in private moments, I should have learned something. I should know what to do. But maybe that's my curse, my punishment for whatever

I screwed up in my past life. I can see the world but never really be part of it, never live honestly. And what kind of relationship survives on secrets and lies? I can feel my stomach turning thousands of meters below. I'm not sure if it's the thin air, the ambiance of the stars, or the romance movies Sayuri used to drag me to, but part of me is thinking I shouldn't go down without a fight.

I stretch back to Earth, determined to set things right. I snake through the university botanical gardens and bite through the stems of cabbage roses, the thorns threatening to puncture my lips as I carry the flowers in my mouth. When Sayuri comes back in the morning, I'm waiting for her. I don't want to waste anytime. The moment she walks through the door, I take her into my arms and kiss her neck, her ears and tell her things will be different. No more secrets. She takes the flowers and looks at them, and, for a second, I almost expect her to light up, but she closes her eyes, and when she opens them, they're red and filled with tears. I lean into kiss her, but she pushes past me and locks her bedroom door. I bang on it a few times, begging her to let me in before I give up and retreat to the living room. I flip through channels, not really wanting to settle on anything. People are disgustingly happy on television. When she wakes up a few hours later for work, she pretends I'm not even there.

So, it's come to this. After Sayuri leaves, I peek out the window and watch her walking down the street. I wait a couple of minutes, so there's a reasonable buffer between us and stretch my neck out the kitchen window, laying low on the sidewalk, skimming the surface like a hovercraft. I'm out in the open, and it's lighted out with all the street lamps in the neighborhood, but I don't really care. If someone sees me, I'll say, "Fine evening for a hallucination isn't it?" and who wouldn't believe they were hallucinating? At least long enough for me to hide anyway. Around the corner, a silver Jaguar is idling, but I can't get a good look at the driver from where I'm situated. Sayuri walks over to it and gets in. My face is burning, and I almost forget to follow the car as it drives off. I'm moving down the road with the speed of an aging marathon runner—fast but just enough to tail them a few meters behind. My sadness quickly turns into jealousy and rage, and by the time the silver Jaguar stops at the Grand Hotel, I really want to do something to the car.

Behind a hedge, I wait for him and Sayuri to leave the garage. I've seen this guy before—a real pretty boy. He's one of those men that wear cowboy boots and tight pants and spend half their paychecks on perms, trying to wolf up their hair. He has his arms around Sayuri as they walk inside, and if it weren't for the security cameras near the entrance, I'd slither over there and bite his ass off. As soon as it's clear, I pick up the sharpest rock I can find and scratch and chip away at the Jag. My mouth's sore from holding the rock so tightly, and I'm tired and sweaty from all the effort. I swing to the side of the hotel and peek through all the windows until I find one with a view of the front desk. And there, beneath the amber glow of the lobby's chandelier, he's holding my wife. She's smiling, laughing. She's absolutely aglow, and I can't even remember the last time I saw Sayuri like this. He runs his fingers over her lips before kissing her, and she doesn't hesitate to kiss him back. I can't look away, but I'm not angry, jealous, or even sad at this particular moment. I feel numb, and the only thing going through my head is: How could I let this happen? How, after spending half a lifetime watching people, could I not know what to do?

I picture waiting for Sayuri back home, my neck hovering over the living room as she walks in, her trembling hands pointing house keys at me like a weapon. I take the keys away and wrap her tight within my arms, the arch of my neck and the proximity of our bodies forming half a heart. I tell her it's me. She whimpers and let's out a weak, "Oh." I hold onto this silent image of us, caught between truths, until our bodies are enveloped in darkness, as I pull away from the window and glide onto the nighttime streets, watching my wife's figure become fainter and fainter until I can't see her at all.

Place a flower in one hand and a weapon of your choosing in the other.

Go to the bathroom and stare into the mirror. Continue to stare with minimal blinking until you cannot recognize yourself.

Stare at a friend. Continue to stare until you cannot recognize your friend

Girl Zero

Our daughter, Kaede, has returned to us five years after the police fished her out of the community pool, her body sodden and distended like the carcass of a baby seal when I identified her in the morgue. But now, she looks just as she did the day she disappeared: her hair pulled back tightly in a ponytail, a front tooth still growing in to fill a gap, her knees bruised from playing on the ground. She has not said one word since I returned with her three days ago, stares vacantly as if she is engaged in a task like counting blemishes on the wall or how many times a person opens their mouth when not eating or speaking.

After another day of silence, we take her to the hospital we were told to go to if any problems arose. My wife, Yumiko, carries our daughter, rag doll-limp, from examination room to examination room, only releasing Kaede when a radiologist needs to run an MRI. Yumiko holds her hands up to the control room glass. I hang back in the doorway, studying the images on the monitors. The words "abnormality" and "mental impairment" thicken the sterile air, just as they did after doctors breathed life into Kaede's tiny, blue body after Yumiko delivered her three months too early.

"Is everything okay?" Yumiko asks the technician.

"You'll have to wait for the doctor," he says.

She turns to me. "I wish somebody would tell us something," she says. "Why are they running so many tests?"

Inside the scanner, Kaede is catatonic, expressionless. Her eyes do not waver, do not flit nervously like flies. "They just want to be thorough," I answer. "It's not like what we did to get her back is exactly common. You have no idea what I had to do to find any Yokai at all…let alone the right kind. We have to make sure that's her in there."

"It's her. That's our girl."

"I hope so."

"What is that supposed to mean?"

Yumiko never cared to know the details of what I did. The only thing that mattered was that I returned with her daughter. In the month after the cremation, I moved into a capsule hotel, realizing my wife needed more space than my sleeping downstairs could provide. The last thing Yumiko said to me before I left was, "This wasn't supposed to happen." I just wanted to make things right. And then one night, I read a news article about Rokurokubi, demons with human faces who have the ability to stretch their neck to extreme lengths, being involved in a bank robbery. If anything could have helped me, it would be their kind, I thought, the Yokai, the nearly extinct supernatural races of old Japan—miniature people, dragons, flying heads, the stuff of manga and horror movies. As children, we all read about them, collected trading cards with artistic depictions. Parents told cautionary tales to make their kids behave. Like how the Kappa eat little boys and girls who go swimming without supervision. Like ghost children bringing misfortune if toys aren't put away. After coming across documentaries about the terminally ill getting a new lease on life with Yokai assistance, I needed no further convincing that I would do everything I could to bring Kaede back. At first, Yumiko was horrified at the idea, thought I had lost my mind. "And I'm the one who is supposedly unhinged," she said. "You're hunting for magic." But, after a few days, she called. "Try," she whispered, half-asleep. "Bring her back to me."

Yumiko remains silent and watches the monitors. "You wanted this, too. That's her. See?" She points to the shifting MRI images. "Those are her bones. That's her heart. That's her brain."

Dr. Kobayashi enters, carrying binders of old case studies. "Good, good. Doesn't make much of a fuss, does she?" He is trailed by a jaunty, young woman in a pencil skirt and a blond man in a frayed cardigan sweater. The doctor studies the scans. "Healthy, little girl," he says. "Ten fingers. Ten toes. Two lungs. A strong heart like a bongo drum."

"So, she's normal? She's okay?" Yumiko asks.

"Let me put it this way: She appears to be a typical seven-year-old."

"Except..." I add.

"Of course," Dr. Kobayashi continues. "We can't be entirely certain. There have been only six cases of shape shifters replacing humans in the past century. Only three of those were documented in any verifiable way. The rest are closer to legend."

"Fact is, we thought this species was all but extinct," the blond man interrupts. "There is little known about how the Noppera-bō imprint on someone, to what extent."

"And you are?" Yumiko asks.

"I'm sorry," Dr. Kobayashi says. "This is Dr. John Travelstead, a xenobiologist and cryptozoologist from California. Well-known in his field for his work on Bigfoot. And this young woman behind me is Ayui Saito, one of our special-needs child therapists who has some experience with the supernatural."

Yumiko dismisses the American zookeeper, glares at him. "Bigfoot," she whispers to me. "What a joke!" She looks at the young woman again, her slender legs, her silk blouse. My wife runs her hands through her bed hair, rubs out a toothpaste stain on her pilled sweatshirt with a growling tiger on it.

"She seemed to react to photos we've shown her—Disneyland, festival scenes, fireworks. Has she shown any signs of remembering?" asks Ms. Saito.

"Stuffed animal," I answer. "She reached for her panda, Miki." But as much as I want to believe Kaede remembers Miki, I wonder if she held him simply because he's soft and has a gentle face.

"Well, that's a very good sign," Dr. Kobayashi says. "Keep trying to familiarize her with her old life. I'm sure Ms. Saito and Dr. Travelstead both have insights into how to proceed. I wish there were more we could do medically, but, as I've said, we have very little precedent." He squeezes Yumiko's shoulder, shakes my hand, and leaves the binders with Dr. Travelstead before power walking down the hall.

§

"Let's let her choose," Ms. Saito says. She offers a tray to Kaede and gently nudges her forward like a chick on its first flight. Kaede wanders the cafeteria, looking back often for reassurance. She stares for long periods at each item, poking at the plastic wrap on pastries, testing the weight of fruit cups. The fridge, full of soft drinks and juices, is of special fascination. She opens the door and runs her face across the cool bottles, breathes in deeply. Kaede returns, trying to balance several candy bars, two donuts, a container of noodles, a rice ball, and a styrofoam take-out box filled with a little of each beverage on her tray. She shuffles her feet and stops whenever she sees an item about to topple to the ground. She furrows her brow. Her cat-like wailing that has caught the attention of the room sounds as if she is saying, *Whoa, Whoa, Whoa.*

"Chocolate." Ms. Saito picks up a candy bar from the tray. "Does she like chocolate?"

"What kind of question is that? What kid doesn't like chocolate?" Yumiko answers. She nudges my arm.

Ms. Saito opens up a Lotte Crunky Crunch Chocolate bar and breaks off a couple of pieces for herself and Kaede. "We're trying to figure out if she remembers being a kid," she explains. "She went for the candy first. The question is did she remember that? Or was she just attracted to the bright packaging?"

I can tell Yumiko just wants to get out of here, that she's not buying the expertise of what she referred to as government ghost-busters. The longer we're at the hospital, the harder it's going to be for her to ignore that we're not here for a routine pediatric check-up. For Yumiko, it is not a matter of who or what but when—when will Kaede be the girl who collects cicada wings in buckets, watches old cartoons with her mom late at night, laughs at monkeys at the zoo until her sides hurt.

"So, you just asked villagers about local legends?" Dr. Travelstead asks. He leads me across the cafeteria to a quiet table. The televisions mounted on the walls are playing an anime movie about a girl who can jump through time.

"Old women, children, police, anyone who would stop for me," I answer. "An old school teacher pointed to Ryusen-Do Cave in Iwate Prefecture, said there were places deep within the Earth where these things hid, trying to hang onto life. You have to understand, however, that it took over a year of dead ends to locate any usable information at all. The people in these small villages protect their secrets; maybe the teacher felt sorry for me."

Dr. Travelstead scratches his head, creating a flurry of dandruff. Part of me is unsettled by the American's appearance, a stereotypi-cal crackpot who might very well live in an apartment covered with news clippings and blurry photos of the Loch Ness Monster. But, in trying to bring back Kaede over the past few years, I've been pretty much alone. I'm grateful for any help these doctors might be able

to provide. Dr. Travelstead flips through the much abridged report
I gave to the authorities after I emerged from the forest.

"Tell me," Dr. Travelstead says. "This can't be all of it."

"To be honest, I'm still coming to terms with what happened,"
I say.

"We're here to help your daughter," he says.

I nod, knowing I don't really have a choice if we want to get
answers, if we want the government to stamp a piece of paper that
says Kaede is A-okay. And so I tell him how I dove through the
cave's lakes, which possessed an unnatural clarity as if I were falling through glass, how I felt my way along the mossy edges for a
corridor. Seven times I came up for air, swallowing mouthfuls of
water in the process, until I found an opening barely large enough
for me to swim through. The cave complex was like a subterranean
Venice—natural limestone cathedrals, bridges, vaulted ceilings all
punctuated with a labyrinth of water. I ran a piece of fishing line
behind me, so I wouldn't get lost, left red glow sticks in crevices like
bread crumbs. For all I knew, I'd just find a forgotten beach full of
blind, glowing insects like the ones you see on nature documentaries, gangs of stalagmites and stalactites my only company. At first,
there was just rock, ancient air. Just darkness save for my headlight.
The sound of a waterfall plunging even deeper into the Earth. And
then I saw them tucked in an alcove: alabaster, smooth like marble,
huddled together on top of each other, their limbs intertwined,
tangled like the night crawlers my father used to put in buckets
when we went fishing. They breathed in unison, the mound of their
mannequin bodies pulsating. Hairless. Faceless. Genderless. As I
approached, they began to separate from their pile into individual
creatures, each standing at what had to be over seven feet tall. How
they knew I was there without eyes, ears, a nose, or a mouth, I did
not know. Perhaps they sensed motion, the subtleties of light vs.

dark. Perhaps they could hear my thoughts—the way I clutched to my mail-order hunting knife, my fear about this place not meant for humans. There were seventeen of them.

Dr. Travelstead catches up with his notes, pushing up his glasses between lines. I wait, observing children with their families, children coughing, sneezing, clutching their parents, playing with toys and Pokemon cards. These kids, like anybody else, are collections of memories. Kaede is sitting stiff as board, staring at the food Ms. Saito and my wife are holding in front of her. The girl I brought back may very well be a blank slate. She doesn't remember the deer in Nara stealing her rice crackers before she could feed them, how I chased a peacock at the Honolulu Zoo just so she could have a feather. If she never recovers moments like these, will she really be the same girl? She'll look like her, maybe sound like her. I'll say goodnight, and I love you. And really try to mean it. There's fear certainly that something wrong will happen, but there's also the possibility that maybe, just maybe Kaede has a second chance to become the person she could never have been, the girl that Yumiko and I envisioned before she was born that would play volleyball like her mother, attend a prestigious university.

I had a lock of Kaede's hair with me that I collected from a brush. I wasn't entirely sure what to do or how the creatures operated. I stepped closer and the creatures followed suit. I stepped to the left, the right, and they followed. I held out the lock of Kaede's hair and slowly moved closer. The creature closest to me reached out, grasping indiscriminately, an infant searching for a nipple. I tossed the lock, and it clutched the hair to its chest. The creature began shaking so quickly that it seemed to disappear at times. Its once stone-like body, impenetrable and sculpted, transformed into a translucent jelly, ribbons of light dancing within, coalescing into organs, veins, bone. Its body shrank in size to that of a child, Kaede, her features becoming more and more apparent. And then another creature took hold of this new daughter and another took hold of that creature and so on, until a chain had been formed, and I realized that there would soon be seventeen of her.

"Seventeen? What happened to them?"

I've said enough for now. I close my eyes and see seventeen of my little girls staring at me—naked, bewildered, not quite complete. I can feel their tiny hands grasping at my clothes, as I tried to shield Kaede #1 from the others, as if she were purer, less of an impostor. I change my mind about telling the whole truth—at least for now. Perhaps by saying it out loud, I'll have to admit what happened, and I'm not quite ready for that. "There are many places to hide down there," I say.

"Do you think any might still be alive?"

"I don't think so," I answer. "I couldn't imagine it."

Kaede approaches and rests her head on my shoulder. Yumiko smiles, delighted at the thought of her little girl remembering how much she loves hugs. I place an arm around her, cautiously, as if any more force would break her. While I don't want to be afraid of my daughter, I can't help but fear that she'll somehow steal away a part of me if I touch her. I try to ignore thoughts like these, but in dreams, I imagine waking up, looking in the mirror to see my head resting on Kaede's tiny body, her hands as my hands. Yumiko pulls a wet wipe from her purse and cleans our daughter's mouth, littered with crumbs.

Yumiko looks up at the doctors. "Have you two decided that she's not going to transform into Godzilla?"

Dr. Travelstead pushes up his glasses for the millionth time.

"I think the only thing we have to worry about is eating too much candy," says Ms. Saito. "But we will be checking in periodically.

Home visits. Just to see how Kaede is adjusting, if there are any unforeseen incidents," Dr. Travelstead adds. "Government require-ment, as you know."

"You're not convinced that she's our daughter," Yumiko says.

"I didn't say that," Dr. Travelstead answers. "But you said yourself that the color of her eyes changed, that her bruises disappeared."

"I like her new eyes. And the disappearance of her bruises is a good thing."

"Of course," says Ms. Saito. "We just want to monitor her to be on the safe side. She's a very special girl."

"We can work out a schedule later," says Dr. Travelstead. "But I want to clarify your information. There are two addresses listed…"

"I haven't lived in our house for some time," I explain. "But I'm nearby, so…"

"Maybe you should come home for the time being," Yumiko interrupts. "You should be home for Kaede."

We've had our home in Toyama for over ten years, ever since Yumiko wanted to try for children, leaving our closet of an apart-ment in Osaka for someplace quieter. She worked at a small travel agency, and I accepted a supervisor job at the Kurobe Dam and came home damp and smelling of grease and sweat. We made fran-tic love in the shower in those early days, our bodies pressed hard against tile, the grime of my body circling at our feet. We spent the rest of our evenings talking about the child who could be in our lives, listing names, imagining their future—a scientist? A baseball player? Maybe a veterinarian?

After Kaede was born, robbed of six minutes of air as she entered the world, Yumiko's eighteen-year plan transformed into taking things day-by-day. We celebrated the little achievements—a bike ride, coloring within the lines, performing as a lion cub in a play.

If Kaede liked to do anything, she liked to move. Non-stop. Full-speed. Her special education program held dance classes, she took gymnastics with her mother twice a week, and if it were up to her, Kaede would have lived her whole life on a swing, watching the world go by in a blur. When a public pool opened down the street, conversations were had about whether or not Kaede was ready, if it was safe. Kaede looked out the window every day at children marching down the street in brightly colored swimsuits. She thought water wings were magical devices that would allow her to glide through water like a mermaid. "It's pool time!" she would tell us repeatedly. "Pool time, pool time!"

After several more months of begging, a heavy snowfall, and an ill-timed nap, I awoke to an empty house on a Saturday morning, the television still blaring Miyazaki's *Ponyo* that I had put on for my daughter. I searched the neighborhood in house slippers—the backyards of strangers, playgrounds covered in snowdrifts, toy shops, and convenience stores. It did not occur to me, being shuttered for winter, that she would go to the pool, that her body could squeeze through the iron gates, as I walked past them. Every little girl on the street with a pony tail became my daughter. I called Yumiko, who had been running errands, repeating two words: She's gone.

§

Kaede wakes up nestled between her me and her mother. My eyelids are cracked open, and I watch her study her room that we've covered with photos and posters—Kaede with her best friend Kazuka posing with Goofy at Tokyo Disney, her grandmother in a pillow fort, the temple gardens of Kyoto set aflame in the fall with foliage. Perhaps she is trying to remember the sounds Yumiko made when she pointed to each one: fend, bah-san, dinneylan, koto. Does she know the girl in the photos that looks like her is her? I'd like to think that the memories are simply blurred in her mind as if she is looking back in time from beneath water, and that, with our help, this water will drain.

"Morning, kitty cat," Yumiko says, rubbing our daughter's tummy. Yumiko shakes my shoulder, unaware that all three of us have been awake for over an hour. "Get her ready. I'll make breakfast."

I lift Kaede out of bed and raise my arms in the air, waiting for Kaede to do the same, so I can help her out of her night shirt. I carry her to the bathroom, suddenly reminded of how I brought her out of the wilderness. My daughter seems transfixed by the shower. But when I guide her closer, she squirms and inches back. She curls toward the wall and clenches a towel rod for security. I stick an arm under the water to show her there's nothing to be afraid of, and try to coax her again. "It's okay, see?" Kaede screams when I try to lift her. She screams when I try to comfort her. She escapes the bathroom, naked and crying.

"What the hell are you doing to her?" Yumiko yells from downstairs. She runs to find Kaede, blowing past me.

"She was afraid of the water," I explain. "I didn't do anything!"

I hear my wife rustling in our bedroom.

"It's okay," she says. "You don't have to go in the shower. It's okay. Come to me." She carries Kaede downstairs to the yard and fetches a cloth and a bowl of water. I follow them, feeling like I let my wife down again and led our daughter to a little death. I notice the perfection of my daughter's skin, soft like an infant, absent of blemishes and scars, as Yumiko rubs the towel in small, circular motions. Kaede studies her mother: soaking the cloth, ringing it out, placing the dampness on her body. Does she remember drowning in the pool? Does she remember the cave's lake? If that's the case, I can't blame her for running. For her, maybe just thinking about water of any appreciable amount unsettles her, makes her want every feature on her body to disappear, so nothing can get in.

After breakfast, Yumiko sets aside home movies, Kaede's educational toy computer with math and English programs, and vocabulary flashcards with cartoon pictures on them. She flashes the cards to Kaede and slowly pronounces each word (once in English and once in Japanese): Buta, Pig; inu, dog; toshokan, library; gakko, school. I look on, observing my daughter's lips moving whenever Yumiko speaks, trying to sound out the words (or perhaps just imitating her mother). "Don't over-do it," I say. "It's not all going to come back at once."

Hours later, Kaede is pointing to the flashcards and doing a pretty good job of sounding out the words. She is busy on her toy computer adding apples, subtracting kittens from baskets. It took the old Kaede her entire life to master any of this. If she remembers how much she wanted to be a dinosaur or that the reason she's supposed to hate the color purple is because Akiko, a girl from down the street who called her stupid, likes purple remains to be seen. But the new Kaede knows that $2 + 2 = 4$. She even knows that 2×2 also equals 4 and that $4 \times 4 = 16$ even though the old Kaede never finished the computer programs let alone mastering multiplication. "No, no, go slower," Yumiko says. "You're supposed to go slower!"

"What's the matter?" I say. "She's doing great."

"I know what's best for her," Yumiko answers. "I know what she's capable of; it isn't right." She takes away the flashcards and the computer and gives our daughter crayons and some paper. Kaede looks confused and is probably wondering if she has done something wrong. She stares and tilts her head like a befuddled dog. Yumiko draws a pink stick figure mother with a triangle skirt holding hands with a little stick figure daughter. Kaede picks up a crayon and, in a maelstrom of spirals, completely coats the paper black.

§

By the end of the week, Yumiko has planned a tour of Kaede's childhood: the special education center, her favorite playground, visits with old teachers and friends. I pack the Corolla with juice boxes and rice balls, and I'm hoping my wife will be forced to admit our daughter isn't the same person she once was after she sees Kaede in her old stomping grounds, face-to-face with playmates that are now practically teenagers. My daughter hasn't really spoken yet, but I know this Kaede is capable of much more—the math problems on her computer, reading a cookbook and fetching ingredients for her mother from the fridge without being asked, even sitting still for the entire duration of a movie. I see Kaede in the rear-view mirror, soaking in everything we pass, her tiny hands pressed against the window.

Yumiko turns back frequently to check if her little girl still has her seatbelt buckled, if she's paying attention to the landmarks her mother is pointing out. "That's the Mr. Donut your cousin, Haruka, works at. There's the toy shop you get your puffy stickers from," she says, analyzing her daughter's face for some form of recognition. Kaede nods her head, and I wonder if she's agreeing because she understands or remembers or if she's figured out that nodding makes her mother smile and sometimes results in her being let off the hook from pointing at pictures.

"What did you tell them?" I ask. I turn into the parking lot of the Super Kids Special Needs Center where Kaede is scheduled to meet her old teacher, Yamashita-sensei, and her best friend Kazuka. There is a mural alongside the building with portraits of every student holding hands under a rainbow. Kaede is near the center and a pigeon is resting on her shoulder.

"What do you mean?" says Yumiko. "I told them Kaede has returned and wants to visit."

I shut off the engine and glance at the center's playground just a few feet away from where I used to pick up Kaede after work. I can almost see her, waving to me from the top of the curvy slide.

"They were both at the funeral," I say. "They know what we did."

"Of course," she says. "Of course they do."

Kazuka pushes Kaede on a swing and talks about life in the center's junior high program for kids with ADD, about the boy who is not really her boyfriend. I feel sorry for Kazuka, for putting her in this situation. I bet she's doing all she can to forget about the funeral, how much she cried when she tried to tell me how much Kaede meant to her. She can't help but compare her body to Kaede's, which resembled her own at that age but now probably seems so genderless and delicate like skin wrapped around twigs. And I'm sure she wonders if they still would be best friends if it weren't for the accident, how they would fit into each other's lives. Certainly, Kaede's mental abilities would have paved an entirely different adolescence from Kazuka's, which apparently has become increasingly about school, boys, and swimming.

Kaede closes her eyes as the swing goes higher and higher. The old Kaede liked the feel of the wind on her face, the way her sandaled feet raked the sand beneath her like a zen garden.

Yamashita-sensei watches the girls with us. Having lost her own daughter to leukemia two years prior, we feel a kinship with her. I can't imagine what she must be thinking, watching Kaede again, all the whys, hows, and is it rights.

"The two girls were inseparable," she says. "They called the sandbox their kingdom."

Yumiko smiles. I remember Kaede talking about castle pass-words, about how she and Kazuka were princesses of the play-ground. Yumiko does not see or perhaps chooses not to acknowl-edge Yamashita-sensei's trembling hands or the way Kaede's friend has not smiled or laughed once since seeing our daughter.

Suddenly we hear the swing chains jangle and the cries of Kaede sprawled out on the ground. Kazuka is examining her. I can see that Kaede's lips are dotted with crescents of blood, her right knee a trellis of torn skin. Kazuka takes a tissue packet out from her pocket and dabs the wounds, noticing the grown-ups have already mobilized and are looming behind her. Kaede's wounds, like invis-ible zippers, begin to close.

Yumiko takes Kaede into her arms.

"Did you fall?" she asks. "Looks like you're okay, big girl. Not a scratch on you."

Kaede raises her arms to be carried.

Yamashita-sensei backs away slowly and sits on the swing.

I concentrate on Kazuka, her mouth hanging open in a state of shock, still holding onto the tissues she used to compress my daughter's now non-existent cuts. I hold out a hand and gesture to the tissues, and she hands them over.

"She was hurt," Kazuka says.

"I know," I answer.

"She's okay, honey," Yumiko says. "Don't worry. She's fine."

As Yumiko's tour of Kaede's childhood continues, I can't help but think about what happened on the playground. What if the injury had been more serious? If she loses a limb, will another grow back like a starfish? What are the limits? When Yumiko is away with Kaede, observing one of her old ballet classes, I call Dr. Travelstead about what happened. And I tell him, someone, finally, about how, when the

sixteen other Kaedes intended to follow me out of the cave like a pro-
cession of ducklings, I had no choice but to stop them. I don't know
how to say this, I said. You have to understand. After all, I couldn't
very well have sixteen copies of my daughter running around the
countryside. One after the other, I held them under the cave's stream.
I tried not to look at their faces as their tiny bodies struggled, their
fingers digging into my arms. And one-by-one, I pushed them over
the waterfall, some of them having changed into the creatures they
once were, glowing like fireflies as they descended into the darkness.

§

"What's the story with the cucumber and eggplant animals?"
Dr. Travelstead asks. Yumiko didn't plan on inviting the doctors
over to our house for the Obon holiday, but I insisted, said it would
be good for them to see Kaede at a family gathering. She smiles
disingenuously. What she really wants to tell him is to get the hell
out of her house.

"They're for the spirits of our ancestors to travel on to and from
our home. It's an old tradition," she answers. Ms. Saito looks at the
family photos on the wall.

"It's a family holiday," Ms. Saito interrupts. "Maybe like Thanks-
giving in America without turkey. Not many Japanese people have
big ovens."

Dr. Travelstead and Ms. Saito are studying Kaede's every move-
ment across the table without trying to be too obvious about it. She's
sitting in my lap as we watch television with her uncles and aunts.
She is gnawing on a KFC drumstick while watching Iron Man fly
over New York.

"How has she been?" Ms. Saito finally cuts to the chase. "I know
there was an incident at her old school a few days ago."

"She just fell," Yumiko says. "She's been fine. Adjusting very well as you can see."

"Your husband said her hair color changed temporarily from black to light brown the other day," Dr. Travelstead says.

"He exaggerates," Yumiko answers.

I shake my head.

"Who is your favorite Avenger?" Uncle Toru asks Kaede. Toru picks up a chicken skewer and cleans it off with one bite. "Magic trick," he says. He pours another Sapporo into his glass.

"She doesn't really speak," I explain. "She hasn't spoken yet."

"Why not?" asks Aunt Tamami. "Your wife said she was getting better."

"She's getting used to things," I say.

"But she's not like before," says Aunt Tamami.

"No, she's not like before," I say.

"That's what you get for fooling with those Yokai," Uncle Toru says.

"Is she still…you know?" Aunt Tamami says in a hushed tone while pointing at her head.

I ignore her last comment, fixate on the amount of make-up she has caked on her face, the fact that she is sitting in the seiza position in high-heels, her stilettos digging into her not insignificant backside.

I'm certain Kaede knows they are talking about her, understands that they think she is wrong somehow, that I look at her differently than her mother. She cocks her head when people say her name, looks like she is processing everything. Does she want nothing more than to be who she's supposed to be? Does she want to be more? I've seen signs that some memories are coming back to her. She typed *(^_^)* into my cell phone one day. She drew a picture of a little stick figure girl in a pool. She is embarrassed by her shapeshifting, knows it is something that her mother doesn't like. But I've seen her control it when she thinks no one is around, like when she was looking at Yumiko's fashion magazine and changed her skin tone to mimic blush. Does she wish she could talk? Does she know why she can't? And what would she choose to say first?: I want more cheese, I love you, don't change the station, don't be afraid, I'm a smart girl, I am Kaede.

"We think that the creature didn't fully imprint on your daughter because it didn't have a live sample; you used her hair," Dr. Travelstead explains to me in the driveway. Ms. Saito walks out of the house and waves goodbye. "There are obviously pieces of your daughter in there. But she's learning about the world all over again."

"Learning faster," I add. "What about her scrapes on the playground? the shifting?"

"Monitor it, call us." Dr. Travelstead shakes his head. "These aren't necessarily bad things at the moment. But we don't know if they'll stop one day, if they'll somehow become dangerous. From what you've told me, it would seem the Noppera-bo revert to their native state when their life is threatened. We're still looking for the other sixteen you told us about. It's preservation. Other shifts might be caused by stress, hormones."

"But she's still a little girl," Ms. Saito says. "She could be very important for science one day. But wherever she came from, that's what she is now."

"I know," I say. "But—" Where is the guidebook for all of this? What if something terrible does happen?

Ms. Saito hugs me unexpectedly. Dr. Travelstead shakes my hand and squeezes my shoulders. He offers his closed fist in solidarity and says he's available 24/7 for Kaede.

And with two friendly honks, they leave.

§

For the next couple of weeks, Kaede seems to be fine—physically speaking. I have not observed any shifts. Yumiko is still coaching our daughter to be her old self and has started taking her to gymnastics classes again. But Kaede has been having bad dreams ever since she watched a documentary about bats. Flashes of her origin have lingered in her memory, popping up in her drawings. She draws the cave over and over again. Sometimes she wakes up in cold sweats, shaking, pointing to the drawings. The dreams seem to be getting worse, and each time something is added to her drawing repertoire, a little more about where she came from and who she is supposed to be—me holding the sixteen others down, the birthday she got a princess costume, me crying after what I had done, falling into the pool and dying. On this night, we hear her whimpering. But the whimpers quickly turn into screams.

When Yumiko and I rush to check on Kaede, we see her only in silhouette, her features, her skin, her pixie ears have disappeared, even her fingers and toes have fused together into a smooth clump. Her skin has the consistency of a jellyfish, punctuated with light. Our daughter has become a mannequin of stars.

"Tatsu!" Yumiko screams. She races to Kaede's side but is afraid to touch her. "Can you hear me? Are you there? Little girl!"

I stand in the doorway, silent. My eyes follow the points of light shooting through Kaede's body like comets, imagining them to be parts of my daughter's spirit. I know Yumiko wouldn't be able to survive losing her again. I know I wouldn't be able to either.

"What's happening to her?" she says. "Is she coming back?"

"I don't know," I say. "I don't know what to do. Maybe we should call Travelstead?"

Yumiko studies her daughter and shakes her head.

"No, wait," she says. "Don't do that. We don't know what they'll do. I don't want them taking her away."

We watch over Kaede, as the light from her body casts nebulae across the walls, our faces. We sit at the foot of our daughter's futon for hours until her body begins to fade, and her skin returns to normal. Her fingers become distinguished, her face is built up like a sculptor molding clay. And then she opens her eyes, which have emerged as if they rose from beneath water, and begins to cry.

"Mommy," Kaede says. "Daddy." Her beautiful, beautiful voice.

We take our daughter into our arms.

"You're okay," Yumiko says. "You're home."

"What happened?" Kaede asks.

"Nothing," I answer without hesitating. I look at my wife and we grasp each other's hands. "You just had a nightmare," I say, knowing that Kaede probably knows this to be untrue.

My daughter has come back. She holds us and tells us I love you mommy and daddy, and she asks if we can sleep with her tonight, if we can go out for pancakes tomorrow morning. She is Kaede again (Kaede plus) and that's all that matters this very moment. I tell her she can have all the pancakes she can eat. I ask her if she remembers anything. She asks for a story and for more hugs. And then she says, "There was black, but then I could see everybody from before and everyone after. I could go swimming in a forever ocean. I was made of light."

When checking for the ripeness of fruit at your local grocery, be attentive and tender. Pay attention to texture and firmness, the sound in your hands. A rotten fruit may be grumpy and surly, grunting when squeezed. A moderately ripe fruit will hum pleasantly. A ripe fruit will moan in ecstasy, tremble in your palms. Press firmly with the tips of your fingers. Work your way around. Repeat as needed.

The Peach Boy

And so came the day when Momotaro, whose parents found him inside of a peach, grew tired of adventures and settled down with a samurai's daughter. For years they found happiness, planting peach trees on their land, telling stories to each other—her tales of warriors on horseback wearing masks of monsters, his tales of demons, of fellowships forged with talking bees, mill stones, and crabs. But while their lives were seemingly full, the samurai's daughter felt an emptiness in the house. And so every year they tried, in vain, to have a child. Each birth came too early, the samurai's daughter producing a peach pit with the face of a crying boy or girl. She placed the pits on shelves alongside name cards—Misora, Eiko, Manabu, Ayu, Sachiko, Matsue, Hirano, Yoshi, Suzume, and prayed for their spirits every night. More and more shelves were built but with every pit added to the wall, the samurai's daughter's melancholy grew deeper, until, at six months in again, she heard a heavy plop in the outhouse and made a decision to stop collecting her pits entirely.

One day, Momotaro, while clearing the outhouse, discovered that a peach tree had begun to grow. He took the sapling, cleaned it off, and planted it in front of their house. And seeing how the pits on the shelves only saddened his wife, he asked her if he could try planting those as well. "Let them grow," he said. "Let them live." She hesitantly agreed, so long as he didn't take them all at once. So, one-by-one he planted peach trees as gifts, outside the homes of his neighbors.

Rain storms came and went, the laughter of children in the summer had come and gone until those children weren't children at all. At long last, the first peaches had begun to grow, and the village waited in anticipation of harvest. On Official Peach Day, a holiday declared by the local samurai, families brought out baskets to collect the first fruit, sinking their teeth into a juicy peach or two as they worked. What the villagers had noticed, however, is that each tree, while being perfectly unremarkable otherwise, possessed one gargantuan peach that equaled at least a dozen or more of a standard size.

"This big one is enough for dinner," one man remarked.

"My children will have a lot of fun sharing this," a woman said.

That night, as families sat down to enjoy their bounty, the giant peaches began to rock back and forth. An infestation, many thought—worms, rodents. Eat around the ruined parts, a mother told her children; we can't afford to waste. The children cut into the peach with knives, with their bare hands. They stuffed their faces and smiled. And then, suddenly, the eating stopped. They could hear crying. One child could see an outline of a mouth beneath the peach flesh, another could make out a finger. The mother carefully removed the rest of the fruit and uncovered a healthy baby girl. In the next house, a bachelor held a baby boy, in the house of a widower crying could be heard, and in the home of Momotaro, the samurai's daughter was filled with joy. She cradled her son, Hayato, looked up to her husband and said: "Find the rest of my children. Bring them back to me."

Ten Things You Should Have Known Before You Died

[Text Unavailable to the Living]

The Inn of the Dead's Orientation for Being a Japanese Ghost

You're born and live your life but then the unexpected happens (or, for some, the end is just what they had planned): You sleep surrounded by family, listen to the hum of asystole from a hospital bed, feel a sharp pain in your chest as you drive home, take your first and last breath as you exit your mother; you swallow your wife's pills, walk calmly into freeway traffic with a note taped to your shirt, slip your fingers into 9mm wounds, wrap a bed sheet around your neck to break your fall beneath the shadow of Mt. Fuji. You've probably heard my story, or some movie version of it—poisoned with face cream by a woman who wanted my betrothed, my man asking his friend to rape me, so he could toss me away with shame, my hands, upon seeing my sagging face like melted clay, grabbing a sword and puncturing my throat, cursing those who had messed with this soon to be demon bitch as the tatami turned red. Yes, I am Oiwa, the grudge with never-ending hair, and I am the keeper of the Inn of the Dead. Welcome!

Inn FAQ:

When you died, you found yourself in a whole lot of nothing—black, silent, goes on forever. It's the universe's waiting room, where the higher ups decide if a reikon (your spirit) moves on, rots in Yomi, or gets sent to a place like this—basically another waiting room. You also might be wondering why we're all Japanese, why the afterlife isn't more cosmopolitan as it should be. Certainly, there are places where the dead mingle sans national borders, but I've found that it's just easier keeping things in the club at first—after all, Japanese ghosts (and make no mistake about it, you wouldn't be here if you weren't going to be chucked back) are some of the most bad ass ghosts in the world.

The Inn of the Dead, a traditional *Ryokan*, has been imagined into existence by some of the leading craftsman of the Edo period with a recent renovation by Masako Hayashi, one of the country's first female architects. (Note: I do consider myself a feminist and support dead professional women as much as I can.) The Inn adjusts to fit the needs of our guests, so we are never out of rooms, ice, or towels. While we serve traditional food such as miso and soba, guests can request just about anything from any time period and culture— mead, KFC, a decent bratwurst. And yes, for you newcomers, the answer is that we don't have to eat. But where is the fun in that? Outside, the Inn boasts a swimming pool, an onsen, a deck with several tables, and an observation area where guests can take in a breathtaking view of the horizon of the celestial plane. Important: Please do not leave the inn grounds under any circumstances or your spirit will be lost for eternity.

Your First Visit:

The first thing to understand is what you are not. Natural deaths and accident victims who had happy-go-lucky lives? These are the dead that let shit happen and rolled with it. You, my friends, didn't roll with it. For whatever reason, you felt cheated, interrupted, or just plain fucked with the hand you were dealt, and this tore the soul of your soul out, barring you from moving on. Another soul? Yes, it's like how quarks and gluons are at the heart of atoms; there's always another layer. Perhaps you were killed for love like me or left a child behind who can't cope without you or died during a heated argument with the manager of a Tokyo Denny's who was diddling your wife. In any case, you're pissed, unhappy, and restless.

The duration of your initial visit is unknown. Some stay for months or years while others are gone after a few hours. The length of your stay can be affected by the following:

1. Recognition of the type of ghost you will become (followed by adequate preparation)
2. The Disturbance of someone, something, or someplace on Earth that is connected to you
3. How pissed off or sad you are

A: Me? I never even left the house where I was killed until a Shinto priest sent me packing.

A: Foreigners who die in Japan must remain in the void before being transported to the afterlife that is right for them. We're not haters but this Ryokan is exclusively for Japanese ghosts, for Yūrei.

A: According to my records your husband survived the car crash.

A: According to my records your son was too well-adjusted to come here. He went straight to the light.

A: I can never completely move on.

You, of course, may return to the Inn whenever you like, so long as you don't make a habit of it. Some find they are ill equipped to haunt and require more preparation, time to compare notes with others. Others simply need a break after a few hundred years—sit down and catch up on what's been going on with the world, drink a cup of coffee, have ghost sex (Advice: Read "Knock 'em Dead: The G-Spot of the Afterlife"). In rare cases, ghosts are able to "follow the light" in which case their spirits may return for thanks (but most fly out of their haunts like a bat out of hell). In even rarer cases, ghosts are exorcised and are sent back permanently (see our staff directory).

The primary responsibilities for newcomers is to figure out what or who you want to be when you return to the world—Will your skin be blue? Will you be prone to walking like a spider? Will you smell like rotten eggs or the perfume you used to wear? Will they be able to touch you? Some of this is of your choosing and some of it is tied to how you expired. To help you in this endeavor, the inn holds workshops, break-out sessions, and support groups daily, tailored to particular flavors of hauntings (i.e. "Bathroom Cliches: Subverting Expectations of Mirrors and Shower Curtains" and "Hopping in the Sack: How to Spoon your Human". Enclosed in your packets you will find a brief introduction to our more common ghosts. Do look within yourselves while we go over these together.

Yūrei 1: Ubume—Women who have died in childbirth

Perhaps it is fitting that we begin with those who came here while bringing life to the world. This particular flavor of ghost is one of the oldest and was quite prevalent until modern medicine. But I should note that not all Ubume are spirits of the dead. An occasional few are, in fact, manifestations of the emotion tied to the loss of a child. Some will appear pale and bloodied while others will look no different from those around them. Traditionally, Ubume would ask someone if they could hold their swaddled baby. The baby soon becomes increasingly difficult to hold until it is revealed to be not a child but a large stone. We've left this folklorish nonsense behind thankfully—women these days demand satisfaction and know what they want. This can take the form of the following:

1) Caring for a child (in conjunction with his or her parents)—kids are suckers for floating toys
2) Caring for a child (while driving away or killing his or her parents)—parents aren't fond of writing on the walls...especially in blood
3) Killing a child—avoid cutting so as to preserve that angel face

Common Locales: Maternity wards, schools, family homes, playgrounds

Case Study: Michiko Takahashi, Osaka (1974-2012): Died on the way to the hospital in the back of a taxi. Stalks new parents. Kills and replaces hired nannies. Develops friendship with the child. Drives a wedge between child and parent. Drives a wedge between husband and wife. Appears in dreams of child as angelic figure. Appears in dreams of husband as sexual fantasy. Appears in dreams of wife as demon. Leaves with child. Walks into the ocean with child.

A: It's not that we shed human morals in death. We certainly know that we shouldn't murder or kidnap. But none of you would be here if you weren't wronged in someway. And sometimes, as a spirit, a being ruled by emotions, morality is a distant luxury.

A: How do I live with myself knowing what I've done? 1) They had it coming. 2) They started it. 3) I may have been a bit of a demon bitch before I died.

Yūrei 2: Zashiki-warashi—Ghost Children

Children are cute. Dead children are just plain creepy. Zashiki-warashi can be the spirits of children, supernatural entities that take the form of children, and the spirits of adults who have, for whatever reason (mommy or daddy issues, a desire for some serious playtime), taken the form of a child. As with living children, there are good seeds and bad seeds. Some spirits will bring a house fortune and joy, some will delight in causing harmless mischief (stealing socks from the dryer, scraping out the cream filling in Oreos), and an increasing number these days are just plain throwing shit fits—terrorizing innocent families, killing other children for eternal playmates, resetting digital cable boxes and smart TVs. Psychologists on both sides of the veil have blamed parents for creating an entitled generation. Just last month we had a kid here who demanded to be returned to his body or his dead grandfather, a former Toyota executive, would have words with me. But I also have to point fingers at horror movies for giving ghost brats the bright idea of engaging in tomfoolery like making their skin pale, hiding in closets, and stretching their jaws out to obscene proportions. Just because you can do it doesn't mean you should; you're creepy enough. Of course, I'm not saying there aren't cases where a good old-fashioned haunting isn't in order. But many kids die without having lived enough to be truly pissed. (We're talking decades of an abusive marriage vs. not getting the right colored Power Ranger here.) Enjoy the afterlife. Play with fluffy. Let your parents know you're okay without having them lose their minds and then play kickball on Saturn's rings.

Case Study: Hayato Nishi, Sapporo (1981-1991): Died of asthma attack during school recess due to his emergency inhaler being confiscated by a teacher. Appears light blue to those who can see him (children, chosen adults, those with intermediate to advanced psychic abilities) but is more often heard—wheezing, coughing, crying. Perches above the desk of his former teacher, stalking her throughout the day. Sleeps with his mother. Follows other children to recess. A quiet boy by nature, Hayato is content to watch. His presence creates a tightness in the chests of those near him. He is heard, he is felt within the lungs.

A: *You'd think so… but even after hundreds of years, these kids still retain their childlike demeanor, their wonder and propensity for silliness (and mindless cruelty).*

A: *Oh, they are well-aware of the passage of time. They learn and observe like any of us. But their priorities are always the immediate. The new toy. The new thrill. The family that might stay and take care of them. The playmate who won't be afraid.*

Yūrei 3: Onryō—Women who have been wronged

Let's get one thing straight here; I'm not one of those "I hate men" granola activists (not that there's anything wrong with that). But we have to agree that men have historically screwed over women, overshadowed their accomplishments, silenced them, and abused them. I'm not sure why pissed off Japanese women become so bad ass when they die, but I imagine it has to do something with our culture. We're a quiet bunch generally…and many women (even these days) are still very much in the obedient housewife camp. In other words, there's a lot of shit bottled up. I don't blame younger girls for swearing off marriage entirely. Give me a Corgi and a career. Onryō are spirits of women who have stockpiled enough bullshit from the men in their lives that they have no choice but to come back as angry and disgruntled. Even in death, the lives of these women still revolve around the men that tormented them—no moving on, no heaven, no frolicking in a field of wildflowers. And a lot of them, including myself, couldn't even kill our exes. Torment? sure. But damn if I wouldn't have loved to push him off a cliff. Spirits of this ilk traditionally wore white kimonos and had long, seemingly endless black hair, a look I admittedly contributed to. These days, anything goes—why not look fabulous while sticking it to the man?

Case Study: Makoto Kobayashi, Nagano (1975-2006): Stabbed multiple times and dismembered by her husband who believed she was having an affair with an Australian ESL teacher. Possesses bodies of young, foreign women and seduces their husbands, still in undeserved grief. Reveals her true face mid-coitus. Kills the possessed in front of their husbands by jumping in front of trains. Her reflection is seen in the windows of the passing cars.

Note: This type of ghost is, no doubt, among the most unfortunate. My advice to you, should you find yourself identifying with such a category, is to work it. If you're going to be a vengeful spirit, you might as well be good at it. Spend your hauntee's work day figuring out how to disturb their night. Don't hold back.

A: No, it's not fair . . . to anybody.

A: I don't make the rules; I'm here to explain how things are. If you find some cosmic loophole, you know where to find me.

Yūrei 4: Goryō—The vengeful wealthy (what happens when CEOs
have unfinished business)

Back in the day, these spirits were honorable lords and landowners
who were killed via elaborate (often politically motivated) plots—
think ninjas hopping on rooftops and bushy eye-browed samurai
rumbles. But Goryō in the 21st century can apply to any spirit who
wielded any kind of power and has unfinished business—an uncertain merger, hidden assets, documents that need to be revealed or
stay hidden, opponents who need to be dealt with. Regardless of
how they died, these spirits often manifest themselves in disheveled
formal attire with their mouths stuffed with money and/or documents. Many are the result of suicides. They cannot speak but spend
their time trying to communicate with those that can help them.

Case Study: Kimimitsu Toru, Sendai (1938-1989): Hanged himself from a tree in the Aokigahara forest at the base of Mt. Fuji after discovering a merger with Honda he had spearheaded would result in his termination as CFO of Love Robotics Inc. Controls the prototype bodies of love, maid, and service robots. Killed his replacement in a love hotel with a Miss Harajuku 2000. Delays factory production of designs that were stolen. Appears in the dreams of the board of directors.

A: The Prius brake problem/ recall had nothing to do with Goryō.

A: Yes, the recession hit us hard here as well.

A: Small business owners do come back… but these cases more often resemble familial hauntings and are usually very temporary.

Yūrei 5: Funayūrei—Ghosts at Sea

This is the last category we will cover (of course you can consult our librarian for more information), but I should note that this particular category is of special importance due to the recent tsunami. While most of those lost during this disaster moved on without a hitch, many found themselves where you are right now, in the lobby of the inn. Their lives interrupted, they simply needed more time to find closure. Most of them have followed the light after strolling the land of their no longer existent neighborhoods. But a few stayed, residing near the shore, within the shallows, in the darkest passages of the abyss. In the old days, Funayūrei were depicted by artists and storytellers as being hell-bent on drowning people, capsizing boats, possessing ships, and ravaging fishing villages with tidal waves. And while there are certainly cases of ghost ships, of the occasional dead sailor with a chip on his shoulder who would see your dingy at the bottom of Sea of Japan, most sea ghosts are quite harmless and are, in fact, there to help those in need—a drowning boy, a desperate fisherman, a lone sail boat in need of a gentle push to get home. Some present themselves as they were in life while others have a bit more fun and take the form of giant fish, mermaids, or even entire boats.

Case Study: The Fishing Trawler Columbo, Sea of Japan (2004): An old man, his two grandsons, and a first mate battle a storm off the coast of Niigata City. The father of the boys had been lost to the sea not long before. This time one of the boys is lost, caught in the trawl net, as the boat is pulled under. The Columbo is seen with a man and a boy a year later, warning a family on their yacht to turn back due to an incoming storm. That same year, the Columbo rescues an injured sea turtle and brings it to port. The boat and the crew vanish not long after turning over the turtle to the port authorities.

A: Are mermaids real? Well, no ... and yes. Belief is a strong thing for the living. It's even stronger for the dead.

A: There are most certainly ghost pirate ships.

I'll remain here for further questions but your rooms should be waiting for you should you want a moment alone before our meet-n-greet dinner. I believe we're having a make your own pizza night (but you're not limited to this naturally). Before entering your rooms, simply think about home and you'll be there upon opening the door—your bed, your house frozen in time and space for your personal use. We offer this service during your orientation so that you may better transition to the isolation that is to come when you return home.

A: No one will be able to see, hear, or sense you.

A: When you need to come back, simply open your bedroom door again and think of the Inn.

Again, I'd like to welcome you all to the Inn of the Dead. We know this isn't what you had planned but together we can create a piece of heaven right here. On behalf of all of the staff and our alumni, I offer you a big, hearty Boooooo.

Technique for Deep Sea Diving:

Step 1: Immerse yourself in water regularly. Hold your breath for as long as you can to encourage an aquatic disposition.

Step 2: Drink a mixture of 1 part sea water and 1 part algae until air becomes difficult to breathe. Approximately 2-3 weeks.

Step 3: With the needle of an urchin, cut five slits into your flesh spaced approximately 1.5 inches apart and measuring the length of your palms. The placement of the slits is up to you. (Most choose their neck or lower back.)

Step 4: Wrap slits in kelp and attempt to sleep beneath water in a controlled environment (i.e. a pool filled with sea water, tied to a dock).

Step 5: Dive, dive, dive!

Do not attempt any of the above outside a magical realm. May cause serious injury or death.

The Passage of Time
in the Abyss

Storm clouds drift over the Sea of Japan as if large pieces of char-
coal were dragged across the sky. Ryu, the steersman of the fishing
trawler Columbo, checks the weather forecast on his phone, flipping through the interactive display. They'll be heading toward the
confluence of two storm systems if they leave now. He scratches
the stubble on his cheeks and calls Hori to the wheelhouse. The
two men look out to sea, studying the dark waves, trying to reason
with the knots growing in their stomachs as a bright, multicolored
mass moves across the radar. "It's up to you," says Ryu, "but I don't
recommend we stay out long." Hori turns to look at his grandson,
Tamo, telling old legends to his little brother, Kogi. If the family
didn't need the money so badly, he'd wait until the next day. "Let's
head out," Hori says. "Catches are always best before a storm. We
can always turn back."

§

Urashima Taro walks along the shore and comes upon a turtle
being tortured by a group of children wielding sharpened pieces
of driftwood. The turtle is on its back, flailing. Speckles of dark

95

blood dot the sand around it. Feeling sorry for the turtle, he scares the children away. The following week, a seal approaches Urashima and informs him the turtle he had rescued was, in fact, a princess and she would like to thank him. Urashima clings to the back of the seal and dives past the reaches of sunlight. For a moment, he forgets about his physical constraints, about his need for air and imagines himself in a starless sky. Water begins to seep into his mouth, his nose. He wants to gasp, and finally with a pained grin on his face he does. Suddenly, something grabs hold of him and a stream of warm air is blown into his mouth. He can't see what has him but recognizes the impossible similarity of human fingers wrapped around his arms, of human lips sealed tightly around his own, as he descends deeper into the ocean. Below him, a faint glow emerges within a canyon as if shooting stars had been collected. As the light becomes brighter, Urashima sees that it is a woman who has him—a beautiful woman, wrapped in seaweed.

§

The engine sputters and grinds to a stop, stranding the Columbo in the middle of a shipping lane. "I wish you'd stop telling those stories," says Kogi. "Do you think I'm an idiot? Our father isn't in some underwater palace like Urashima. He's dead. His skeleton is at the bottom of the ocean—fish food, probably a nice little house for baby stingrays and moray eels." Tamo ignores Kogi and continues with the story. It's been five years, but he knows his brother has just become old enough to feel their father's death. A worn picture of their father, taken a few months before he drowned, hangs out-side the wheelhouse. Kogi busies himself double-checking knots and cutting more bait, turning the volume up on his music player. "Dad would have liked the stories," Tamo says under breath, so his brother won't hear. But he hears. "Well, you're a big baby. You're probably the only one in high school that doesn't have hair on his balls." He throws a squid at Tamo but misses.

§

Chinese and Korean cargo ships pass the Columbo at ramming speeds as the rain begins to pour. The leviathans couldn't slow down in time even if they wanted. As a precaution, Ryu radios the larger ships to alter course while Hori fixes the engine, then calls his wife and baby girl to check in—just in case. Ryu sees his family twice a month if he's lucky. He keeps a picture of them under his Tokyo Giants hat next to a flattened pack of Marlboro Menthols...

§

When Kogi used to cry all night, Tamo would tell him their father had gone to live in the Dragon Palace somewhere beneath the sea. He has told him this so many times over the years he almost believes it himself. Marine denizens wander the red coral halls and crystalline chambers, serving the deities of the ocean. Giant sea turtles shuttle members of the royal court throughout the labyrinth complex, through colonnades encrusted with pink and crimson anemones. Each side of the palace is a different season, and one day inside equals one hundred years on land. "I'm sure he wants nothing more than to come back to us," Tamo would explain to Kogi as he fell asleep, "But we would be long dead if he tried."

§

A lone seagull, separated from his flock, heads for land, pumping its wings against the elements. It tries to avoid being pushed by gusts of wind into the rising sea, pulsating like a net interwoven with thousands of beating hearts. A single raindrop lands on Tamo's nose. The plastic wind gauge atop the aerial mast makes a rapid turn and then takes another.

§

Within the walls of the Dragon Palace, sea creatures can choose to take on human form or other forms entirely. As Urashima and the princess stroll the gardens, a group of jellyfish approach the perimeter of the compound, marked by pillars of kelp. Urashima watches their glowing, elegant bodies transform into sacks of human flesh as if all of their bones had been crushed or removed. They drag themselves across the courtyard and move like amoebas, emanating a somber, ritualistic cry. The princess explains that the jellyfish were among her father's first servants; early victims to his infamous rage before old age had calmed him.

§

Hori overhears Tamo as he climbs up from the bowels of the Columbo. Like Tamo, he wants to believe the stories. He pictures his son drifting beneath the waves and looking up at the world he's left, forgetting the truth: that he had to fish parts of his son's body out of the ocean after it had been mangled by propellers; how he dove through the bloodied water, grasping for an arm, a foot, what was left of his son's head, putting what he could find into garbage bags filled with ice until his son's remains could be burned.

§

Ryu taps out a text message to his wife:

what r u doing?...going through a storm. r we meeting next wk?

Caught in the wake of larger ships, the boat rocks and creaks like a wooden cradle. Pots rattle in the galley and the nets on deck sway back and forth like anxious specters. Ryu's phone plays a dance remix of Peter Cetera's "Glory of Love" as a meteorologist on the radio predicts gale force winds and swells of up to seven to ten meters on the radio. The phone reads:

talk l8r -at pilates I < 3 u!

§

Schools of fish appear on the sonar, and Ryu shouts to Hori that they should release the nets before the storm worsens. Tamo lowers the ramp and unlocks the trawl wings while Kogi stands beside the net and bait buckets, preparing to monitor the release with his grandfather. Waves crash onto the ramp like ravenous fingers. And as the Columbo increases speed, the net and bait buckets are pulled off the boat, disappearing under the dark canopy.

§

After spending a few days in the Dragon Palace, Urashima asks the princess to send him back. She gives him a wooden box and instructs him to never open it and then kisses his neck to give him gills for the journey home. Urashima marvels at the lights of deep-sea creatures as he rises from the abyss, standing on the back of a turtle. As they rise, sunlight breaks through the water, reflecting off schools of anchovies. Urashima waves his hands through the mercurial cloud before his head rises above the waves. From afar, it looks as if he is walking on water. The turtle brings him to the same place he had rescued the princess. But everything is different. His boat is gone, all the boats are gone and so are the docks he and the other villagers had built. Instead, all Urashima sees are shining towers rising into the sky and millions of people streaming down endless roads.

§

Sensors on the cod-end of the trawl net send back data to the wheel-house. Fish have begun to fill the net, and Ryu signals Hori who is listening to Tamo's story. Sheets of frigid water flow across the deck. The waves, once lapping gently at the bow of the boat begin to crash against the Columbo, threatening to lift the boat like a giant hand. Hori holds tight to his grandchildren, leading them below deck to take refuge.

§

The streets of Yokohama are frightening to Urashima. Cars are strange, armor-clad carts to him, carrying people at great speeds. Giant, silver birds fly overhead, sending thunder through the skies as they pass. The people on the street are dressed strangely—nearly all of them wearing black, and all seem to be in a rush to go some-where. Urashima walks for hours, following the flow of people through underground walkways, over bridges, and across busy intersections. At a park, he sees a familiar sight—a bronze Buddha, turned green with age. In front of the statue stands a man, who, like Urashima, does not seem to fit in with the surroundings. The man is wearing a thatched conical hat, a simple yukata, and raised wooden slippers as if he were a farmer tending a rice paddy. A murky film covers his eyes and deep canyons run down his sun-burnt skin. In his hand is a wooden cup holding loose change. Urashima asks the farmer for help, trying to explain his situation. The farmer ignores him at first, gazing out into the busy square like the Buddha behind him. "I know the story," the farmer mutters. Urashima furrows his brow. "What story? I'm trying to find my family," Urashima answers. The farmer forces a laugh. "You're very good. But this is my territory. Go panhandle on the other side of the park." Urashima doesn't know what the farmer is talking about. He asks about the story again, if he knows anyone with his family name. The farmer, now uncertain if Urashima is a panhandler and seeing Urashima's obvious distress, decides to humor him: "One day as a fisherman walked along the shore, he came across a turtle being tortured by a group of children..."

§

In the galley of the Columbo, Kogi is playing Final Fantasy while Hori listens to Tamo's story and warms up soba noodles on a hot plate, trying not to splash the sauce as the boat rocks. Hori has been through rough storms before but never with his grandchildren on board. If he could have run the family business without the boys, he would have. He turns to Kogi and prays silently. In the wheelhouse, Ryu watches the waves roll under the bow, making course corrections as needed. He calls his wife, but there's no answer. During their last call, she mentioned an American man who offered to teach her English. Ryu takes the photo of his family out of his hat and mutters "Gaijin bastard" under his breath. On the radio, the Tokyo Giants are beating Hokkaido's Nippon Ham Fighters 5-4.

§

As the farmer tells the story, Urashima tries to understand how the world could possibly know of his journey. Is he creating the story or is the story creating him? "And after hearing the story from the stranger in the park, Urashima fell into a deep sadness over the loss of his wife and daughter, both having died hundreds of years ago," the farmer continues. "He ignored the warnings of the princess and opened the wooden box only to find nothing inside. Wrinkles suddenly appeared on Urashima's body and his bones contorted and grew brittle until they crumbled entirely. And just before Urashima was turned to dust and swept away by the wind, he heard the voice of the princess, telling him that he should not have opened the box for it contained his old age." Urashima looks down at the box the princess had given him. If the story is true, he will certainly die if he opens it. He sits on a stairwell with the box between his feet, scanning the exotic landscape for anything familiar. Hunger eats at his belly. People rush past, paying Urashima no notice. As the sun goes down, the crowds begin to thin. Vagrants with shopping carts and soiled tarps emerge from all directions and set-up camp for the night. Urashima, knowing there is no place for him here, closes his eyes and opens the box. The voice of the princess is carried by the wind…

§

Hori is impressed by Tamo's telling of the legend. Kogi, playing the role of a jealous brother, finds faults in it and boasts he could create a better ending, a challenge to which Tamo double dares him. "OK, you want a story?" Kogi says, after slurping his last soba noodle. He stands up, bracing himself on a counter, almost falling over as the boat rocks, and takes a breath.

§

Ryu takes off his hat and fishes out a crumpled cigarette—his last. The picture of his family, pinned inside, stares back at him as his ears pop from the dropping air pressure. He lights up and checks his phone for messages even though he's been staring at it the entire day. Ryu wants to provide a good life for his family, but feels hurt and suspicious that his wife doesn't seem to miss him. She used to check in. But now Ryu has to chase her down. He taps out a text message on his phone: *checking in. storm picking up. call me.* His thumb hovers over the send button, but he deletes the message and writes: *r u w/ the american?*

§

And after the farmer finishes telling the story, Urashima looks down at the box the princess had given him. Knowing there is no place for him in the modern world, he closes his eyes and lifts the lid. Suddenly, the air becomes difficult for Urashima to breathe. Bright orange scales replace his skin and spiny fins develop on his torso. Vagrants take notice and begin to gather around. Urashima attempts to stand up, reaching out to one of the drifters but falls to the ground, failing to realize his legs have been fused together. His hair falls out. His head begins to flatten like a ball of flour pressed between two hands, and soon, Urashima begins to resemble more fish than man until only his eyes remain as a sign of his human-ity. The vagrants stare in wonderment at the giant fish, flapping helplessly on the concrete. Some of them propose eating it. Others, believing the fish to be a spiritual portent, begin worshipping it, falling to their knees and rubbing Urashima's orange scales. The farmer, feeling sorry for the stranger he just spoke to, recruits others to help carry the great fish to open water. Ten men on each side hoist Urashima over their shoulders, moving solemnly as if they were carrying a palanquin of a deceased ruler. Children point and alert the attention of their mothers. Crowds grow by the hundreds and helicopters fly overhead. By the time Urashima nears the waterfront, the local media has concocted the following headline: *Eco-terrorists recruit homeless into stealing marine research specimens for release.* Warnings are issued over megaphones and boats circle nearby with divers at the ready. The farmer and his men count to three—ichi, ni, san—and drop Urashima off the pier. Urashima darts to the depths, past the reach of the divers, under trawl nets and around giant hooks. He keeps going in the cold, dark space of the abyss until the soft, pulsating lights of jellyfish surround him, guiding him back to the Dragon Palace.

§

A loud crackle from the intercom silences Kogi and he almost falls to the ground as the boat violently leans to the side. Ryu has requested everyone on deck; the weather conditions have escalated dramatically. Swells as large as apartment buildings threaten to capsize the Columbo and waves pull at the trawl net below. Hori and his grandchildren work furiously to bring in the net. Rain beats down like miniature harpoons, stinging their waterlogged faces, their pruned and paper-thin fingers. Beneath their feet, wooden planks creak, and stray lines have become animated, wrapping around legs with ease. Hori shouts orders to his grandchildren through the howl of the storm and runs to fetch life jackets from the wheelhouse.

§

"Mayday, Mayday, Mayday. This is the fishing trawler Columbo at 42 degrees, 33 minutes north and 137 degrees, 27 minutes east. Storm conditions have intensified. Engines have stalled. We have four people on board. Is anybody out here?" Ryu repeats the distress call, as he tries to restart the engine. Hori rushes in and opens a box of emergency gear. He tosses the steersman a life jacket and a deflated rubber raft and squeezes Ryu's shoulder. "I'm going to try and cut the boat free of the net," Hori says. "You take that raft and my grandchildren if it comes to that."

§

Tamo and Kogi brace themselves on whatever they can as they try to haul the trawl net with the winch. The net, filled to capacity, slowly emerges from the black waves, but the winch struggles to pull it on board. A large swell hits the Columbo, and the weight of the net pulls the boat vertical like a white monolith in the middle of the sea. Kogi holds tightly to the winch and cries out to Tamo who has lost his footing. A stray line has wrapped around his ankles, dragging him down the ramp, digging into his flesh. He cries out in pain. Kogi dives toward Tamo, trying to unravel the rope around his ankles already soaked with blood. "Cut the rope!" cries Tamo. "Cut the fucking rope!" Tamo claws helplessly. And then, as if he knows he is going to fall, Tamo looks up at his little brother, a look that says, "It's not your fault. You couldn't have pulled me up anyway. It's OK, and I love you." The winch fails, cables snap, and Kogi scrambles back up the ramp, holding on tight, his body flat against the deck, as another swell tilts the Columbo. When he looks back down the ramp, Tamo is already gone.

§

Hori rushes out of the wheelhouse after the last swell and shakes a sobbing Kogi by the shoulders before diving overboard. He follows the net cables in the darkness with only a chemical glow stick to guide him, probing the water for anything solid until he feels his grandson tangled in the net, Tamo's arms and legs bent at unnatural angles by the lines, his face pressed behind the patchwork of nylon and wire.

§

Water is filling Tamo's lungs and his body is fighting for its life but the more he struggles, the more the net digs into his skin. In the cold of the water, Tamo barely notices the pain from the cuts on his body anymore, but can feel his grandfather pulling at him and the current of the sea across his face. Tamo imagines the Dragon Palace shining brilliantly below, its kelp spires reaching out to him as jellyfish guide his way, and then, shortly after the last bubble of air has risen from his mouth, he imagines nothing at all.

§

With his knife, Hori tries to free Tamo. But the lines are thick, and even as he hacks at the lines, Hori knows it is already too late. Amidst the indigo light of the glow stick hanging around his neck, Hori holds his grandson. He tries to ignore the gashes across Tamo's face, the way the current moves his limbs like a marionette. He stays with Tamo a moment longer, considering holding him like this forever until another large swell passes, pulling Hori deeper into the ocean and tearing his grandson away from him.

§

Kogi scans the water where his grandfather jumped, hoping his brother will return to him. His lips are shaking, and his skin has aged in the downpour. He asks himself if he could have saved his brother, if he should have done something differently. The questions pull at him with the weight of the dark sky. Although he never admitted it to his brother, Kogi dreams about his father every night. Standing alone on deck, he imagines his father standing beside him, whispering the most beautiful of lies in Kogi's ears—that everything will be OK...

§

Ryu is sending another distress call when he sees a towering wave building up on the starboard side. He grabs the raft and heads to the deck, grabbing Kogi as the wave topples the Columbo upside down; the force of the rushing water cracks and shatters the windows of the wheelhouse, sending shards afloat. Peter Cetera's "Glory of Love" begins to play on Ryu's phone; the music continues underwater for another chorus before fizzling out. Holding Kogi's hand, Ryu swims clear of the boat and pulls a red cord on the raft, inflating it and shooting them to the surface.

§

In the distance, Hori can see the raft's flashing distress beacon bobbing over the waves. Kogi sees his grandfather heading towards them and jumps into the water to meet him after tying himself to the raft. Here, in the center of the Sea of Japan, Hori and his youngest grandson cry in each other's arms. Ryu helps them climb aboard and tries the radio again. The three huddle together, holding tight to both the raft and each other as the storm rages.

§

Hours pass until finally the rain stops. Seagulls cry over the calming waves. And as the sun breaks through the ashen clouds, Kogi notices a large mass approaching from beneath the water. At first, he believes he is seeing things, but as the mass climbs to the surface, Hori and Ryu begin to take notice. From beneath the waves, a large sea turtle emerges and draped on its back, as if he were peacefully sleeping, is Tamo. The turtle swims alongside the raft and the two men hoist Tamo up. "Wake up, brother! Wake up!" Kogi yells. And lying in his grandfather's arms, Tamo's eyes begin to open, staring up at sky.

§

The steersman checks the emergency supplies and loads a flare gun in case they see a boat. Lying down, curled into himself, Hori imagines Tamo, drifting into the deepest passages of the abyss, his body mingling with the lost remains of his father. Kogi hangs over the edge of the raft and stares down into the water. He grabs a mask and snorkel from the emergency kit and splashes into the sea, diving deeper with each attempt, hoping his brother is down there somewhere safe, hoping his brother is on his way back to him.

Dream Vacation Checklist:

~~Malaysia~~

~~Mexico~~

~~Cambodia~~

~~India~~

Egypt

Mars

Venus

Moon

~~Antarctica~~

Atlantis

France

Wherever You Have Gone

The Rest of the Way

COMPANION

On our wedding day, you weighed 115 lbs. When you died, you weighed 97. You are now 8.7 cups of ash, and I figure I can make enough 1:25 scale figurines of you from what you've left behind, so we can see the world.

In Tochigi Prefecture, there's a place called Tobu World Square where 140,000 miniature figures are sightseeing at famous landmarks. A boy holds a balloon at the base of the Statue of Liberty. A young couple strolls the gardens of Versailles toward the New York City skyline, toying with the idea of making love behind a carefully manicured privet hedge. An elderly man reads a map as he rests in the shadow of the Parthenon. He's smiling. Perhaps because he's saved up for this trip his entire life. Or maybe he taught seventh grade history for over thirty years and this is the first time he's been able to see the world outside of a textbook.

I try to capture you laughing. But you're angry sometimes, too. Eyebrows raised. Arms crossed. Airports always brought the worst out in us like the time I lost hundreds of dollars playing slots during a Las Vegas layover. Or the time you brought a flight attendant to tears because she demanded that we check our carry-ons even though we had room under the seat. I'm painting your favorite blue dress on now. The one with little pink flowers. Your travel dress.

Elegant. Lightweight. The shawl my mother knitted is draped over your shoulders. Your mouth is pursed, and I imagine us standing in line somewhere. I'll make a figure of myself with an arm reaching out, rubbing your back. Or maybe I'll be flipping through a travel guide, talking about a starred restaurant, oblivious to your frustrations. *You said:* "How can you not be bothered by this?" And glared at a would-be line cutter wearing an I ♥ NY sweatshirt. "I'm going to the bathroom. You better not let anybody cut in front of us."

NARITA

You glance at a young Australian man talking to his mate. He's muscular and tan, and probably surfs every chance he gets. I glance at a pale brunette with headphones on, sitting by the gate. Stand-by. English maybe. Black stockings. Listening to what? classical, jazz, heavy metal hair bands? Punk. In leopard panties. You take my hand unexpectedly as we approach the gate. I smile stupidly at the girl taking my ticket. You notice. We haven't had sex in two months, and when I tried to join you in the shower one night, you jumped out and said we should take a trip somewhere.

There's no room for our figurines at Tobu's Narita exhibit. Only a few model 747s being loaded with luggage, the terminals, and the tarmac busy with service vehicles. But I carve us anyway and imagine us—at security, buying magazines, arguing at the ticket counter, holding hands after we've taken our seats. You lean over me to peer through the window as the plane takes off. Your perfume smells like cinnamon and honey, and I want to kiss your neck. *I said:* "I think we needed this trip."

ANGKOR WAT

After the guided tour, we explored the complex on our own, wandering through the corridors of the lower levels, which represent the underworld, and up to the highest stupas where paradise and enlightenment await. Tourists streamed around us, clicking cameras, carelessly wielding parasols. We maneuvered around photographers—*sumimasen, sumimasen*. Stopped to press a button on a lone traveler's point-and-shoot. But here, there is just us. I quickly place our figures just outside of one of the gates before anyone sees me step over the rope. A few feet of bonsai tree jungle separates Cambodia from the Great Wall of China.

You are pointing at the tree line where I've placed a die-cast macaque holding a Louis Vuitton handbag the size of a button. I am running after the monkey, frozen mid-sprint a few inches from him. Maybe I'll catch him. You had put your bag down for a moment to take a photo of a purple flower growing out of a relief when you noticed the tiny robber creeping closer. You told me to look at the monkey. *Kawaii*, you said and pointed your camera at him. *You screamed:* "The monkey has my purse!"

I ran. The men within earshot ran, as the macaque climbed the temple walls. He sat perched under the giant, stone lip of a Buddha and opened his mouth wide, as if to mock us, exposing his sharp canines. One of the other men tried to entice him with a power bar. "Come down here you piece of shit," I cried. I began climbing the wall. Tried to anyway. But one of the tour guides grabbed my shoulder and pulled me off. *You said:* "Let it go. It's gone." You collapsed next to a sculpture of Vishnu, protector of the world and God of universal order. *I said:* We can replace it. But you explained they didn't make that one anymore.

TAJ MAHAL

No one told us about the crowds and the smell of feet and the beggars and the never ending cycle of getting ripped off by drivers and "official" guides, although we knew, in a theoretical sense, crowds and poverty were part of the fabric of India. The clerk at our hotel in Delhi gave us a corner room for my Hokkaido Fighters hat. A man on a scooter snatched your head scarf as he drove by, nearly pulling you to the ground. A young boy on a moped chased after the thief but lost him in the thickness of Agra. Debarshi. Twelve-years-old. He had a sick mother. (We wanted to believe he had a sick mother.) You wanted to give him as many rupees we could spare. And as I guarded you while you fished through your bag, we both noticed the boy fixating on my shoes, the fact that his feet were bare, dry and cracked as the ground beneath him. We looked at each other, and your eyes said: take off your shoes. And I did without hesitation. I laced the boy up and walked bare foot the rest of the afternoon, feeling India hot against my skin until another boy sold me a pair of sandals. We walked side-by-side, holding each other like we used to in high school, following a man who said he knew a scenic route to the Red Gate.

Of course, at Tobu, none of this exists. There is only the Taj Mahal, the monument of a man's love for his wife. I place our figurines in the vast, manicured garden under the shade of a tree. Here, we are frozen in the conversation we had that afternoon. And I wish we would have stayed there longer, that I would have fought harder, so everything that happened after would cease to be. *You said:*

"Do you think we have that kind of love?

At first I thought we were talking about the architectural wonder behind us but then realized you were staring at a young couple kissing passionately near the reflecting pool.

"Isn't everyone like that at first?"

"We weren't."

"I'm pretty sure we were."

"High school," you said.

"So the first few years we knew each other don't count?" I asked.

"Do you think it's possible to really know what you want when you're that young?"

"And what do you want now?"

"Not this," you said, standing up.

"And this trip?"

"I guess," you began. You stared at the pink, floral flip-flops beside me, my dirty feet, digging into the lawn. "I guess this is a test. To see if there's anything."

I didn't prod any further. I nodded. I said we should get going if we wanted to make it back to the hotel. I could have asked how I was faring. I could have said more. The guide who came with us had disappeared by the time we returned to the gate. We walked fast, ignoring the flank of panhandlers, guides, and vendors, opting instead to find a reliable rickshaw driver that could take us to the train station. A clean-cut man with a Freddie Mercury mustache waved us over. We were so focused on him, on his unusually shiny carriage, and on getting back to our room that we didn't see what was coming. We no longer walked side-by-side. You walked ahead. You took the first step into the street.

SPHINX

And I would have made you take photos of me, crushing the Sphinx with my fingers, nibbling on the beast's backside. There would have been other people, other couples taking similar photos, making the most of the perspective from an observation point. You would tell me I was getting ripped off by a man trying to rent us camels. You would tell me that you really, really could care less about the damn camels. On a tour we would learn about secret chambers that were built beneath the Sphinx that remain a mystery. And before I even spoke, you would tell me that aliens aren't the answer to everything. But what if, what if? My figurine's arms wave wildly. Your figurine looks annoyed, is looking off into the distance where smog meets sand, where the shanties of Cairo punctuate the horizon.

COLOSSEUM

Despite arguing for most the of plane ride, we would make up at the bed and breakfast you picked out, kissing to a peek-a-boo view of St. Peter's Basilica. We would stay in, forgetting about the Segway tour we signed up for (that I signed up for). You would say that it didn't matter that I forgot the travel plan binder you had been putting together for a month, that we would let spontaneity carry us. Maybe you would have said that. Possibly. Or you would have said there was no point dwelling on it, that we would have to make do. Maybe you would have called your sister and told her to go to our apartment, so she could read off your airtight itinerary. We would waste half the day waiting. We wouldn't have time to go inside the Colosseum before it closed, wouldn't see where gladiators waited for their death or glory, where tigers and rhinos would rise to the arena for a hunt. But we would stroll outside of its arches after dining at a Michelin starred rooftop restaurant across the way—Aroma with two glasses of rosé each.

At Tobu (and in Rome), the Colosseum is awash in gold instead of white light, which means somewhere, someone's death sentence has been commuted or rescinded. Or capital punishment has been abolished in a state or province or prefecture or country. I place us beside a lamppost near where the Arch of Constantine would be. My arm is around your waist. You're looking up, pointing. I'm looking right at you.

EIFFEL

I would have said: If you really want to go up there. You would have said: I wouldn't feel like I really experienced Paris if we didn't. We would go in the morning, before the queues got too long, before the forecast brought fog and rain. We would stop on the first level and have an overpriced brunch brought in a picnic basket. I would say: at least drinks were included. I would say: It better not rain when we get up there. I would say: Is this it? I would say: Even though this place is such a romantic cliché, I'm incredibly happy to be here with you. I would say: I love you.

Even at 1:25 scale, the tower is too tall for me to reach the top, so I place us on the balcony of the first level looking out at the New York City skyline with a pair of binoculars. But we would take the lift to the cupola soon after, drink tourist-bait champagne, and ask a Bulgarian man to take our photo twice. First shot: Both of us side-by-side, smiling at the camera. Second shot: Staring into each other's eyes. You crinkling your nose. Me stroking your hair. We would hang the photos in the living room.

TWIN TOWERS

We were sleeping while it happened. I turned on the television while
you prepared breakfast. Got ready for work. Tied the new silk tie
you bought at the mall the day before. You said: Oh my god, look!
You said: America. I said nothing. I watched the headlines scroll
across the screen and sipped on the miso you had warmed. You said:
That was on our itinerary; we were going to go to the observation
deck. You said: Those people. We canceled our trip that year. There
would be another time—later, after all this. You asked: Do we know
anyone in New York?

At Tobu, there's a plaque next to the World Trade Center (1973–
2011). I place us in a crosswalk adjacent to the south tower. We are
surrounded by power suits, fanny packs, taxis, and delivery men
carrying packages. A woman walks her dog. A couple tries to find
themselves on a map. A homeless man sits on a bench. I don't know
what day or what time it is in this snap shot of New York. A few
minutes before the first crash? Seconds? Or is it years or decades?
But like our conversation at the Taj Mahal, the next moment will
never be. I say: Let's catch a Broadway show. I ask: Do you know
where you're going?

THE STREETS OF AGRA

At the Tobu theme park we will continue our travels. But in our bedroom I've recreated it, the Agra street filled with dust and traffic and people and the cacophony of vendors and hustlers. The shiny rickshaw that would have taken us to the train station. A boy who tugged on my shirt. Our figurines are on the edge of the street. You are stepping forward, waving to the driver. Not far away, a man is selling balloons attached to a cart on his bicycle. The balloons along with a stereo blaring music camouflage the approaching bus and the two mopeds speeding alongside it. I've created everybody here in a variety of poses. The balloon man who tried to warn you, waving his arms. You on the ground with your eyes closed. Me holding you to my chest, wailing for help. Me pulling you away from harm, as the bus plowed through the crowded street. I would have asked: Are you okay? And you would have said: I think so. I would have squeezed you so hard then, kissed you. And you would have let me. The driver would take us to the train station and you would rest your head on my shoulders. And I would have said: Maybe that was a test. And we would say other things, too. But not for a while—Not until we got back home. We would remain silent the rest of the way.

ええじゃないか

Ee ja nai ka

Why not?

{Dance}

{Sing}

{Laugh}

{Jump}

{Forget}

Where We Go When All
We Were Is Gone

I'm dancing in Shibuya's Hachiko Square with hundreds of people. We flail wildly, bark at bystanders, and have a general disregard for our well-being. We've been at it for days now, and despite our hunger and thirst, the pain coursing through our bodies as if our veins have been infiltrated by miniature swords, we know we must continue to dance. The world outside of our party is plagued and wretched, but here we are smiling and laughing.

§

An old energy android, one of the many who were freed from nuclear plant service after the wars, asked me why I was waltzing— maybe two hours had passed since I started. I shrugged my shoulders as I twirled and answered, "Why not? It makes just as much sense as anything else. People are hungry but there is no food. We won a war that raged for so long no one remembers how it started. They tell us we are happy but we aren't. But dancing is real. Dancing is now. When I move, I forget. When I jump, I leave the world." By nightfall, the android, whose name is Azuza 2, and I were joined by several others. We danced in the darkness, listening to each other's breathing and footsteps, occasionally bumping into each other. "Is anybody tired?" a banker asked. We shook our heads and our footsteps became more frantic. And then Azuza 2 asked, "How are you humans finding the energy to keep going?" A scientist spouted theories of adrenaline, of the Eden Serum inoculations, designed to reset people's lives after they die in the face of declining birth rates. But I said, "Who's to say how much energy is required? As far as we know we're the first people in history to dance this long."

§

Once our numbers had grown to a palpable size, the city sent guards to speak to a person they called The Choreographer. This, of course, raised questions because there had never been any coordination among our ranks. The crowd murmured, a path was cleared, and fingers were pointed at me. That the dance might turn into a massacre was no doubt a possibility in people's minds. And I realized that what began as an impromptu release had become something, in the eyes of the government, which bore teeth. The captain of the guard, a barrel-chested man with a sculpted beard, squinted as he spoke. "So, you're the one responsible for all this," he said, gesturing to the dancers. What was our mission? Did we have demands? "Still yourselves," he commanded. But we continued to twirl and shake. "Be still," his lieutenant said, not one-second before he grabbed the banker, who, once at rest, transformed into a faceless figure like a marble sculpture before any features had been chiseled—larval, embryonic but with ribbons of light dancing beneath his skin like the aurora. The features of the same forty-three-year-old man emerged but with the unsullied eyes of an infant. His memories? His spirit? Erased. The captain whispered into his headset.

"What is your name?" he asked.

"Oshio, Eri," I answered.

"Captain Yoshida." He handed me a guard headset. "Our eyes. Contact us whenever another falls."

His guards helped the man who used to be the banker to his feet and ushered him away from the party. Captain Yoshida remained a moment longer, watching in silence, as the dancers circled him hand-in-hand, singing.

"We could kill you all here, Oshio-san," he began. "But that would make us unpopular, give the people a reason to hate us, and we can't very well afford to re-educate the entire country all at once. We'll let you have your protest, wait for you to drop one-by-one. It would seem you're all dead anyway. Only the dance is keeping you alive. You'll be reborn like that one, trained to be proper citizens. Perhaps you'll be a better dancer in your next life." He imitated my jig and laughed before walking away and disappearing in the crowd.

§

The streets were mobbed on the day the party began. The stores were packed, too, except for the shelves. In the food dispensary, a queue zigzagged out the door. Customers were only allowed to buy what could fit in the small, metal pails the government provided—half a loaf of bread, a few eggs, a cut of engineered fish, perhaps a handful of rice. The old woman next to me carried her pail along with four nearly spoiled tomatoes in the crook of her arm. Noticing that I had some room, she asked if I would mind doing her a favor.

"Just the produce," she said. "And some extra noodles. I want to make spaghetti for my husband's birthday."

I nodded, and she gave me the credits before I reached the counter. When my turn finally came, I paid for the food and pushed my way out the store and waited for the old woman. I could see her through the window. Tears streamed down her face as she said something to the clerk. The people around her looked at the floor. She stared at me, and although I felt sorry for her, all I could think about was feeding my husband and daughter. This is what we had become. I mouthed I'm so very sorry before turning away and joining the hustle of the street. A few moments later, someone pushed me hard from behind. I felt the metal handle of my pail digging into my palms, sliding down my fingers. And I stood still in the street, empty-handed, as Tokyo moved around me. The old woman joined the dance party four days later. We were beyond apologies. She smiled as she flapped her arms, kicked her feet into the air, and by the next morning, she was reborn.

§

Sometimes I couldn't help but feel guilty for the children who would grow up without the mothers who joined me, for the spouses who sat lonely at home. The friends, the lost loves who watched on the sidelines, debating whether or not to become one of us—if their lives were that bad, if the unknowable future in their second life would be preferable. Everybody around me has a story. The baker lost his grown son to the Arctic Plague and for years walked the same route home, hoping to catch a glimpse of his boy who worked as a records official in city hall. But we only found this out later, when his son tracked down the details of his first life and asked me about his father who had just left our ranks. I didn't know the baker as well as some others. All I could say was that he was kind-hearted, that he gave extra bread when he could, that he was one hell of a dancer.

§

A vendor on the edge of the square sold antique photographs and posters—families at the beach, fields of grass and flowers that didn't seem to end—a world that none of us had ever experienced. I have never left our city, have only heard rumors about life in other states. Other continents, the blue ocean past the gray haze of Tokyo Bay seem like a dream. And I suppose if our dance is to be remembered by history, I would want it to seem like a dream, something a bunch of unhappy people did to make their life a story, a fairy tale, a happy ending (even if only for the duration of how long our feet and hearts could carry us).

§

We try not to look at each other too closely and instead look out into the distance. I can feel the weight of my soiled clothes hanging off my gaunt frame. I choose not to acknowledge my skin, jaundiced and mottled with bruises. The smell is harder to ignore, but I try. To acknowledge the state we are in is to acknowledge the futile aspect of our protest, the reality of its end. Laughter helps, we've found (with the stench and keeping our minds off anything in particular) and so we laugh almost constantly like the mad.

§

The guard headset allows me to be the eyes of the city. And no doubt, someone somewhere is watching the feed. Yesterday and today and tomorrow will be labeled and stored in a file. A reporter might get their hands on the recordings. A historian might use them to write a paper, speculating about causation and motive—hysteria, disease, protest, mass suicide. Or, perhaps, a low-level clerk will one day be ordered to destroy any existence of what happened, and as people die and are reborn, any memory of our dance will be erased. But I have to believe people will see, that the second and third lives of those of us in the square will see, that the few children born this year will see. And so I weave through the crowd, recording as many people as possible.

§

The guards descended upon the square by the end of the second week, cordoning off the surrounding area. Vendors cleared. Barricades were erected at nearby intersections. Captain Yoshida said too many people were joining our party, that the re-education centers were already under enough strain. "But we'll allow family to visit by appointment," he said. "We are not completely unreasonable." His military demeanor had softened since we last met, and I could almost detect sympathy in his voice. And where before family members had largely lingered on the sidelines or never bothered to visit at all, our new isolation encouraged husbands and wives and children and favorite cousins to speak their minds or make their peace. My teenage daughter came first. I told her about how I stole and had been stolen from, how watching our food disappear broke something inside of me. She said she was angry at first but now just missed me. Separated by a chain, we said all the things people are supposed to say when they know they aren't going to see each other again. And then she said, "Dad is still debating about coming. I told him he needs to." I nodded, imagining my husband pacing the streets in a huff. Next to me, the Scientist, the only one of the dancers who had been with me from day one apart from Azuza 2, cried onto his wife's shoulder after hearing his mother died and entered her third life. And in this moment, he allowed his body to stop, and he transformed into a twenty-something year old version of himself with no recollection of the woman in front of him. Others transformed as well. But mostly, there was a lot of silence and distance between the dancers and their loved ones. Whatever we said wouldn't make a difference. Whatever they asked wouldn't have a simple answer. You were either a dancer or you weren't.

§

I have seen so many dancers fall and get back up that I can't help imagine what I'll be like. Would I become, as if by destiny, someone very similar to who I am now? A seamstress with an affinity for old romance novels? Or will an entirely different spirit occupy my body? I could fall in love with my husband all over again, walking past our old house. And he'd take us to all of our favorite haunts, re-create our first date without revealing a damn thing. Or would I have a completely different type? More brawn over brain perhaps. Who will the government say I am? What skills will I be trained in? For an adult sprung onto the world, re-educated without the memories of childhood, I would be utterly naive to history and the cruel subtleties of the world. Everything, at least for a while, would simply just be.

§

My husband patched a call to my headset one night. Dark rings pooled under his eyes. Clusters of pimples had erupted on his face. He made the call from our ancient futon, and I could imagine him in his underwear, the ones with the holes in them that he insisted on keeping because the new synthetic fibers give him a rash.

He told me how he waited for me to come home. How, when he heard the news of what was going on, that he came to the square and watched from afar, too angry and confused and frustrated to come any closer. He said he was afraid that he would pull me out, which would have killed me. He said: "I want you to keep dancing." He said: "I hate you for it." He said: "I miss you." He asked me how I felt, and, because I wanted him to know the truth, I said that at first I felt more alive than I had ever been but, as each day passed, the fire that was keeping me going was stretching my veins, loosening flesh from skin, shriveling my heart and stomach and liver like dried prunes. He asked me if there had been anyone else because he had read stories of dancers having sex, moving from one person to another like a square dance. I answered with an extended silence followed by the fact that I never knew any of their names. I told him they were single-serving love affairs—the romance of a fruit fly. I didn't tell him how one night, a boy young enough to be my son, got behind me, as I swung around my hips. I didn't tell him that I kissed a waitress for two days straight while a farmer who smelled like dirt and thousands of days of hard work stuck his calloused fingers inside of me.

He told me that the government was taking care of the families of the dancers—money and opportunities to keep quiet, to forget that the dance ever happened. I told him to tell our daughter that I loved her.

§

It's been nearly a month now, and our numbers are dwindling. Street barricades have been taken down. The city no longer pays us notice. Azuza 2 is the only one who is dancing at her original pace. Everybody else has slowed to a lull. Some have learned to sleep while swaying, lingering in that space between waking and dreaming. A nurse snores as she rocks back and forth. Across the square, twin

WHERE WE GO WHEN ALL WE WERE IS GONE

brothers drop to the ground, falling over each other. A young man, one of the few people who are awake, turns to me and asks, "How long do we keep going for, ma'am?" I tell him that I'm not in charge, and that no one ever was. I say, "You can stop whenever you want." And with that, he stills his feet and collapses.

§

Our supporters said we were visionaries. Our detractors said we were sick, diseased in heart and mind, and that our spectacle upset the balance of our great society's way of life. I wasn't trying to be anything. But regardless of my intentions, I had become a leader. And maybe one day, long from now (perhaps in my third or fourth life), as I sit in the library as some other woman, I'll read about what I did here and what it meant. But more likely, no one will ever know. It's certainly possible that this has all happened before, that we enter life painfully unaware of who we are and where we came from, slowly coming to a boil only to do it all over again.

§

In what I consider to be my last days or hours or minutes, I imagine the life my family will have after I'm gone. The government will provide my daughter with a nice city job as a librarian, shelving approved books and removing those that fall out of favor until the day she is reborn. My husband's improved pension will allow him to retire early from the heating plant. Perhaps he will always regret not seeing me one last time. Or maybe in a park somewhere, where all the older citizens crowd the lake, he'll meet someone new and marry again, and he'll be happier than he ever was with me. But sometimes, when he is alone, when our daughter visits with her cyborg boyfriend, he'll think of me and the time we danced together in the abandoned Harajuku train station on the night he asked me to marry him. If I never started dancing none of this would be possible. I would have come home without food, telling my family only part of the story, that I had been robbed, and we would have made what little we had stretch over the week. I'd barter the one piece of jewelry I owned, my grandmother's gold heart locket, for a loaf of bread, a piece of rotten fish, and two cans of meat. And my husband and I would grow old together, saying very little.

§

Now there are barely a dozen of us left. We are spread out so much that we practically blend in with the crowds. And I have to wonder, why us? What is it about our lives that have made us linger between this life and the next so much longer than the others? Azuza 2 dances like a human pretending to be a robot. People think she is performing. Children laugh. A man throws her a credit. She has told me that she continues with us because thus far in her immortal life she has seen too much, that she will keep dancing until the world computes. For the homeless, they had nowhere to go, and there is no guarantee their next life will be any better. And, in a way, I suppose a lot of us could say the same thing. Perhaps none of us really had a choice. Maybe this dance party was always destined to happen because the grim state of our lives required it of us. I am afraid that I will wake up and find myself utterly alone without anybody but strangers to tell me who I am, where I am, and what my purpose in life is. I will work and cling to life credit by credit. I will read books that I think are of my choosing. I will stay within the borders of our city because there is nothing else. And maybe one day I'll stop to think. I'll ask questions and more questions. And maybe, eventually, in a moment of frustration and despair, I'll dance.

As I imagine it, Azuza 2 will still be there. There's a chance her memory will have been wiped clean by those that want history to die. But I'd like to think that Azuza will remember who we all were when the party begins again. Our dance would have more context, more at stake, knowing we had done it all before. We could do things differently—recruit more people, more androids, change the system by erasing enough of us and making sure those that were left to re-educate the reborn had a different plan. People would dance in the square, in the streets, in Ueno Park, in Yoyogi Park. They would dance in their homes and in their cubicles. Dance in the ruins of temples and stadiums and amusement parks. I can feel my feet burning, my legs buckling, as I imagine my rebirth into a world that is our own to create. In multitudes, we would reset—entire districts and neighborhoods of the faceless—larval janitors, secretaries, train conductors. And as I fall to the ground, as my heart fails to pump the last of my tired blood, I imagine opening my eyes for the first time. I am walking down a quiet expressway, navigating around the reborn, headed out of the city in search of a place to call home.

雪女

Yuki Onna
(Snow Woman)

Class Cancelled Due to Snow

The Snow Baby

On a lone mountain, the snow baby melts in its mother's arms. The snow baby has no gender, no face; its body is three snow balls. The mother weeps. She is covered in sheets of ice, her poor, melted snow baby. The mother makes a new snow baby; she pokes out eyes, draws a smile with her fingers. The mother wishes every night for her snow baby to come to life, for her snow baby to speak. The snow baby's ice crystals become bone and blood and skin. The snow baby opens its eyes and cries. The snow baby has a penis, shriveled, retreating from winter. The snow baby curls his fingers around his mother's fingers. Born of three snow balls, the snow baby is round and chubby, a pale buddha. The mother tells stories of her late husband, the hunter, to the snow baby. She tells him of her son, the fisherman, who drowned. The snow baby says *mama*. The snow baby says the word for powdery snow. The snow baby says the word for slushy snow. The snow baby says the word for snow that is good for building. The snow baby says the word for snow that makes a crunching sound. The snow baby walks, follows his mother for firewood and squirrel. The snow baby slides down hills on sheets of bark, over and over again. The snow baby laughs when he falls. The snow baby sticks his tongue out to catch the drops falling from melting icicles. The snow baby is becoming increasingly thin like the melting icicles. The snow baby's skin is like jelly. The snow baby's bones creak when he runs. The mother feeds the snow baby hot stew, which only makes the snow baby feel worse. The snow baby cries in fractals. He cries because a hole has melted in his stomach. The snow baby wants to play more. The snow baby says *mama*. The snow baby says *hurt*. The snow baby is too thin to walk. The snow baby is too thin to speak. The snow baby's body is the width of a young tree. The snow baby's body is the width of the mother's arm. The snow baby's body is a twig, a reed, a blade of grass. The mother rests the snow baby on her palms. The snow baby is a strand of hair. The snow baby is spider silk. The snow baby is too small to be seen. Winter has come on the lone mountain again—the snow baby is three snow balls. The snow baby is quiet and still, resting beside its mother. The snow baby's heart is a snow flake and then two and then three.... The snow baby's heart beats the ice around it into flesh. The snow baby is...

Kappa Conservancy Inc.

Did you know there are only 700 Kappa (aka Kawataro, Komahaki, Kawako) left in the wild? Agricultural runoff, nuclear plant leaks, construction projects, and urban pollution have put these ancient, magical creatures at risk.

For just ¥100 (~ $1.00) a month, you can sponsor a Kappa as part of our Adopt-a-Kappa program. Your contributions will go toward food, medical care if needed, and efforts to preserve pristine aquatic habitats.

HEADWATER LLC

Bottled at the Source

Masa takes a deep bow as Yoko holds a plastic bottle beneath him, waiting for the water to drain from his bowl shaped head like a tea garden waterfall. A trainee at Headwater Bottled Refreshments stands behind Masa with a hose, filling his head up to the brim after he finishes his bow. "We have to wait five minutes before filling more bottles," Yoko says, "The water needs time to change." The frosted, glass walls of the factory are like clouds hovering over the river outside at dawn. Below Masa, on the cold linoleum floor, his childlike ankles are shackled with chains. The trainee shuffles to the lounge to smoke. Yoko picks up a tray of sliced cucumbers and hand feeds Masa, avoiding his forlorn and tired eyes.

Situated in the same village that Yoko grew up in, on the same plot of fertile land that her parents had once farmed rice, Headwater's ganglion network of hallways is located almost entirely underground. Its only marker on the surface is a ten-story funnel, open to the sky like a monumental Victrola. It is the heart of the company according to the Headwater blog and not the Kappa, the mythical, amphibious creatures of Japan with pools of water in their heads that grace the company's anime logo.

Erectile dysfunction, Seasonal Affective Disorder, male pattern baldness—newscasters list the seemingly endless miracle cures from customer testimonials around the world. "They somehow drugged it," says a representative of AquaLuv, one of Headwater's competitors. "People are looting stores, gangs are dealing bottles on the street. No one loves water that much."

In vast, desiccated oceans of sand and heat, Bedouins attest to happier camels and less arduous journeys. Headwater is the official drink of the Olympics, NASA, Japan League baseball and nearly every teenage pop idol, believing their breasts will grow larger if they pour Headwater over themselves in music videos. Headwater, as it slogan reads, is health, vitality and a better life.

Orientation

Yoko reviews the company rules, projected on both walls of the outside corridor, to the trainee. One: Do not drink the water, Two: Always wear your I.D. badge, Three: Leaving company grounds is strictly forbidden without permission (failure to comply will result in termination), Four: All contact with the outside world will be monitored, Five: Do not become emotionally attached to your Kappa, Six: Never leave a full head of water in your Kappa unattended, Seven: Failure to meet quotas will result in reduced leisure and food rations, and Eight: Reproduction of these regulations in any form is prohibited.

Yoko can already tell why this one was recruited, as the trainee reads Regulation Eight again and throws his notes into the dust box. She has gone through hundreds of trainees over the years, including the chief executive officers of the company—her childhood friends and partners in founding Headwater. There are over 500 Kappa in the facility, producing an average of 25,000 bottles per day and 700,000 bottles every month with the aid of over 2,000 residential employees—bottlers, security guards, cooks, doctors and custodial staff.

"Why can't we leave water in their head?" the trainee asks. Yoko tells him to read the chapters in his employee manual about Kappa anatomy and customs. It explains the Kappa, being aquatic by nature, receive strength from water, but due to an ingrained sense of etiquette, must reciprocate gestures of politeness (even under duress) such as bowing, forcing them to spill their magically infused water, becoming weak and docile. Headwater left unattended for too long has resulted in escape attempts.

Yoko keeps her eyes fixed on Masa's beak-like mouth. She thinks of the conversations she had with him as a child, tromping through rice paddies, chasing cranes and storks, collecting the dried shells of dead cicadas. She thinks about the new policies ordered by her partners: heavy chains, torn out tongues, more lies and cameras. Lies to Yoko, lies to the employees, lies large enough to cover nations.

"It's okay. I forgive you," Yoko imagines Masa saying to her. "You tried."

Company Mythos

Beads of light descend through the blue water of the volcanic lake like fallen angels. The water has been talked about for centuries: the source of a princess' beauty, the unquenchable thirst of a prince after eating a fish from the lake. Wooden signs warned of the mythical Kappa lurking in local waters, stories of them stealing children and impregnating women—explanations far more favorable than wartime rape and abortion. Mountains created by Gods, trees planted by ancestors, simple people and simple lives. This is the village that Yoko grew up in. Yoko often walked around the caldera brim of the lake, far past her home and the school she went to. The natural, mossy silence comforted her and made her feel, for brief moments, as if she belonged to the world.

Here, in another age, people sent paper lanterns afloat to deliver the dead to the other side. Here, the nearly extinct creatures of old Japan remained hidden, watching their existence become myth, watching a sad, little girl kick her feet in crystal waters, pulling apart her image like a warped mirror.

Tangible Assets

From beneath the water, Masa would examine, Yoko's elfin toes—each as round and white as a miniature rice ball. He had become fascinated with her. And although the other Kappa had been talking about nibbling on Yoko, as it had been such a long time since they've eaten a human child, Masa was not among them. He broke the rule that had kept all old creatures safe from the new world, and floated to the surface. Yoko saw the Franciscan fringe of his hair, surrounding a pool of water like a birds nest fallen from a tree and then the emerald skin of Masa's forehead. In one of his webbed hands, he held a single lily like a champagne glass. He nodded his head in greeting and water from his head spilled into the flower. Yoko, afraid at first, giggled, bowed back, and introduced herself.

"I'm Yoko."

"Masami. Please call me Masa."

His voice escaped his mouth like a parrot or a ventriloquist, disembodied and hollow. Brown patches of hair circled his wrists. Beneath his brow, his eyes looked like smooth, dark stones.

Yoko took the lily from Masa's outstretched hand and examined it, smelling the water inside. Masa motioned her to drink but Yoko hesitated, remembering stories about Kappa playing tricks on people. After much thought, she took careful sips from the flower, sucking the remaining droplets off the petals and licking the corners of her mouth after she had finished.

"It's really good," she said.

Nearby a Praying Mantis climbed a branch and embraced a caterpillar. She became more aware of her surroundings—the pattering of distant footsteps, the sticky odor of freshly steamed rice at a nearby restaurant. Everything in her body seemed charged.

"Can you feel it?" he asked

Masa came closer, and Yoko could see the subtle wrinkles of his iguana-like skin, the shiny, reflections of his eyes. His three spun-out fingers with their little talons, picked up Yoko's hands, examining each finger. She saw him gazing at the top of her head, and Yoko untied the blue ribbon from her hair and made it into a bow around Masa's wrist.

"My sister gave me this but you can keep it. I have others," she said.

He admired the blue material, holding up his arm to the sunlight. "The others might be angry."

"There are others?"

"Not many. There used to be thousands of us. But that was a long time ago."

Yoko smiles. Masa bows again, refilling the flower and dunks himself underwater to replenish his head. He does not yet tell Yoko the reason why he came to the surface—that the waters have become polluted and his kind are suffering from a painful disease. "You must drink quickly. The water changes into something else if you wait too long; you won't be able to stop drinking it," he says. Yoko nods her head, tips the flower to her lips and closes her eyes.

Founding Partners

"So, you want to be one of us, right?" Haruka said. She was one of those girls that didn't really need make-up to be pretty but wore tons of it anyway. Her hips seemed to always be shifted to one side, arms akimbo with glittery nails tapping at her thighs.

Since high school started, Yoko had found herself without a voice, eating her homemade lunches in bathroom stalls, although what she wanted more than anything was to be one of these girls. How she admired their clothes, the way boys looked at them, how they were everything she was not. She would have done anything to sit at their lunch table, and the only ticket she had was Masa's water.

"Well, to be one of us, you need a bag. We're the LV girls, and no one can hang out with us without something Louis Vuitton," Maiko said. Maiko was the follower and, Yoko thought, anorexic.

"So, you don't have money, and I can't imagine businessmen paying you to keep them company. But you have your supposed little friend and that water," Haruka said. She twinkled her fingers at the lakeshore. "Introduce us. I've been dying for another drink anyway."

"You promise not to tell or give the water to other people?" Yoko asked.

Haruka and Maiko held up their pinkies and interlocked them— a pinky swear.

Yoko turned around and took a cucumber, a Kappa's favorite food, out of her backpack and sat at the edge of the water. A part of her hoped Masa wouldn't surface, while another part felt the towering legs of her new social circle looming behind her like gigantic, hungry crows.

But Masa surfaced and Maiko and Haruka drank water from his head, and because he trusted friends of Yoko, Masa told them stories of his kind. He told them how a Samurai lord had enslaved many Kappa, using the drug-like qualities of stored headwater, to control villagers and soldiers. He told them how a Kappa's power on land is his water, how the waters have become dirty, making the Kappa sick.

Haruka slipped out a pack of Lucky 7's and offered one to Yoko, lit her up and waited for her to inhale. Yoko began coughing. Maiko and Haruka laughed.

"Like a drug—huh?" Haruka said. "People really fought over it?" Masa nodded his head.

"How many of you guys are there?" Maiko asked, "Maybe we can help you." Masa remained silent, detecting a disingenuous air around Maiko, uncertain if he should say anything more. The two girls turned back to Yoko, who was trying to decide how to hold a cigarette. Yoko glanced back at Masa, his hands outstretched and open like a wounded deity. "How many?" Maiko asked again.

Development

In the coming months, the high school basketball and soccer teams would take orders from Maiko and Haruka, assembling at the lake and local rivers after school. At night, they baited homemade traps with cucumber and set them in the water, waiting in matching tracksuits as if they were a synchronized fishing team. The Kappa, hidden from the world for centuries, could not resist the prospect of food in their weakened state. Thanks to Masa, who had been kept locked in a storage space downtown, Maiko and Haruka now knew the Kappa would soon have no choice but to surface or die at the bottom of the lake.

The LV girls had started to amass a small fortune. They gave out samples, rented more storage spaces and walked the red light districts of Tokyo and Osaka. Their teachers at school were the first to be addicted—they wrote notes, made up stories about field trips and called parents. Then came the assisted bathhouses, brothels and strip clubs—they all wanted water, and their customers always came back for more.

Yoko always sat far away in the darkness with her LV backpack when they caught Kappa. A seventeen-year-old wannabe Yakuza stood guard over her with a convenience store switchblade, ensuring she caused no trouble. She pulled out clumps of moist grass and stacked the tufts to make a miniature pyramid. Whenever she looked up, she imagined Masa chained up and alone. His skin was chapped, and all the water inside him ran through his body and into a puddle around his feet as if he were a flower turned upside down to dry. This is how Kappa cry—through pores in their feet. He held out a closed hand toward her and slowly opened it. Inside, rested the ribbon Yoko had given him.

Now it is time to fill more bottles again, and the trainee assumes his position behind Masa, ready to fill his head with lake water. Yoko takes a tray of open bottles and places it on a small conveyer belt under Masa, running back and forth, and bows. And as her body remains bent, she stares at the water streaming from Masa's head, pouring into the bottles until they are completely full. She imagines herself, years ago, swimming with Masa to the bottom of the lake as he whispered stories in her ear and breathed strands of bubbles into her mouth.

Naturally Distilled

As they descended past the curtains of sunlight and into the untouched darkness of the lake, Yoko felt as if she was leaving the waters known to the world and falling into something else entirely. Masa guided her hands, pointing at the other Kappa darting through the water with the speed of minnows; some of their bodies covered in bulbous tumors.

Occasionally, Yoko looked up, and tiny pearls escaped from the corners of her mouth, shooting up to the surface. All sounds seemed to be swallowed except for Masa's voice. There were no dragon lovers at the bottom of the lake as in the myths.

"That's just an old story," Masa said. "Older than us."

"Are any of the stories true?"

"Some."

Masa and Yoko set down on a rocky ledge and suddenly, several Kappa surrounded them, and Yoko thought: They don't want me here. They want to hurt me. But Masa waved his hand and one by one they left. Staring out into the blue expanse, he began telling Yoko about a tiny boy, even smaller than her, who lived long ago and married a princess.

"The three-centimeter Samurai!" Yoko tried to motion with her hands, slicing the water with an imaginary sword.

Masa nodded and explained that a Kappa, an old friend of his, befriended the tiny boy, and because the boy and princess ruled justly, many Kappa served their court. But stories of their headwater spread through the villages, and the boy tricked the Kappa into giving him their water, using it to expand his land, slowly controlling other territories as people became addicted. Only when Kublai Khan tried to invade and the country was preoccupied with defense from the Mongols, did the Kappa escape and go into hiding.

A heavy shower came down on the lake and Yoko and Masa rose back to the surface, gazing at the raindrops hitting the water like miniature harpoons. "You remind me of the princess," Masa said. "She wanted to help us."

Personal Archives

Since Maiko and Haruka stopped pretending Yoko's partnership in the company mattered to them at all, Yoko's days and nights have been filled with elaborate plans to set Masa and the other Kappa free. She draws maps, scribbles notes in a made-up secret code and tucks them into the stuffing of her pillow. Unable to rescue Masa herself before the Headwater facility was built, Yoko knows, that for any plan to succeed, she would need help.

The Scenario: Having garnered support from sympathizers in the company, Yoko will free Masa from his chains as her supporters free as many Kappa as possible. They will do this on the day when delivery trucks are scheduled to pick up bottles for distribution. Because Yoko will need to prove her loyalty to the company, so Maiko and Haruka will let their guard down, Yoko will suggest packaging the water bottles in large, wooden crates instead of the pallets they've been using. She will suggest this not only because Headwater shipments have become prone to highway robbery, but also because the Kappa will need to be hidden during transport and wooden crates seemed like as good an idea as any. The truck drivers will not suspect a thing. Yoko and her supporters will hide in crates with the Kapa until they have passed company grounds. Then they will creep out and sneak behind the drivers, holding syringes filled with tranquilizers and knock them out cold while the caravan stops for gas. The Kappa will run from the trucks like animals from a burning forest while the turncoat Headwater employees guide them to the river, leading to the ocean and to their freedom.

Of course, none of this will ever happen. Yoko always realizes this when she has lunch in the cafeteria and sees how happy the employees are to be at Headwater. She realizes the only people the company hires are those with nothing left on the outside—those without families, futures or minds of their own. What she doesn't realize but probably knows in some little way is the gunshots she hears are not solely reserved for crazed customers who try to break into the facility, but are also for employees that have had enough of the good life underground. Yoko wishes she had done something sooner. She can hardly understand the choices she made as a teenager anymore, why she didn't take Masa's hand and run before it was too late.

Resignation

Maiko and Haruka,
We've known each other a long time, but I've realized we were never the friends I wanted us to be years ago. When Headwater officially became a business, you both said we were equal partners, although now I know you only said that so I'd believe I had the power to manage how the Kappa were treated. I'm not proud of the choices I've made. I've betrayed, perhaps, the only friend I've ever had. I can no longer be a part of this company. The only reason I've stayed for so long is because I've been afraid what you'd do to me if I left. I'm taking Masa (Kappa #001) with me. I will not expose the company but will be forced to if you try to follow us.

Yoko

Yoko stares at the letter she wrote last night, knowing if she puts it on Haruka or Maiko's desk, her and Masa's little bodies will discover what exactly happens to employees that leave the facility. She folds the paper in two, sticks it into her front pocket and dismisses the trainee after he returns from the bathroom. Masa has been crying—there's a large puddle where he stands. Yoko mops the floor, takes a small towel and pats Masa's feet dry. When she's done, she pulls up a stool and takes a blue ribbon out of her pocket not unlike the one she gave him when she was a child and ties it around one of his wrists.

"How are we going to get out of this one?" Yoko says, looking into Masa's expressionless eyes. She gets another tray of cucumber and hand feeds him slice by slice and begins telling him a story about a kappa and a princess that escape a dark fortress. They run through rice fields during a typhoon and shoot through rivers like Earth-bound stars until they get to an endless sea. And when they get there, she tells him how they keep going deeper into the blue abyss as their bodies shrink into hazy, infinitesimal dots until they are completely gone.

Sky Fantastic Festival Bulletin:
Because collecting fireflies can be time
consuming, enlist help from others in
your neighborhood. Just one full Mason
jar per household in a district is enough
to build at least two completely organic
fireworks. In response to concerns
regarding harm to the insects, we assure
you that we take every precaution to
ensure the safety of the fireflies before,
during, and after launches.

Kenta's Posthumous Chrysanthemum

The moment my son, Kenta, died, I was looking up at a point in the evening sky. We call it the Suwari, the maximum height where our fire flower shell would seem to freeze in the air before it burst into what we hoped would be the largest chrysanthemum in Japanese history. Thousands of flickering paper lanterns floated in Matsushima Bay, consoling the spirits of loved ones past and giving the water an amber glow as they floated between the dozens of pine-clad islands dotting the bay and out into the Pacific like reaching fingertips. I assisted Kenta on the launch barge and could see my wife, Ayano, weaving between the crowds on the beach with my little girl, Seira. I suppose I felt something then, an ocean wind too dry for the moist summers of Japan blowing across my face, its static charge raising the hairs on my arms. I could see everyone looking at the sky when the first blast came, searching for the trail of smoke. Kenta cradled his sides in pain, and I told him to get off the barge. Then came the second blast and then the screams, as I jumped into the bay carrying my son, diving into the colored water.

§

When I first taught Kenta how to make stars, he was barely twelve years old. His mother wouldn't let him mix the chemical powders, but he already knew to produce the deepest blues, by far the hardest color to achieve, you needed just the right proportions of Potassium Percholate, Copper Oxide and Red Gum. I'd take his hands and guide them through each step—coating grains of rice with wet powder, carefully laying the wet grains to dry then coating them again as if we were gradually growing a collection of miniature planets. I'd explain to Kenta that the explosions we create in the sky all start with a grain of rice and that this is how we too had come to exist. He'd always grin when I told him things like this. He wanted to be an astronomer or an astronaut but his difficulty with numbers would eventually make this dream impossible. The stars that we made at our family home and factory was the closest he was able to get.

Outside, I can hear Seira talking to her mother. It didn't take long for Ayano to leave our house and move in with her parents, taking Seira with her. She said it was too much for her, being in this place. She said the walls smelled of him and the air within them smelled of the day he died.

"Sometimes I see him," she said, the night before she left. Her voice was faint and unworldly as if she was speaking from the bottom of a dark, kelp forest. I never told her then, but I saw him as well. I had dreams of Kenta falling lifeless in the water. His eyes were open, watching as he fell. For a moment, he almost seemed peaceful. And then, as if he were choking, he cocked his head back, and I saw a blue glow rising in him, up through his chest and throat and out his mouth as if he had vomited the planet Neptune into the sea. The planet floated away, following the orange lights of the lanterns above, guiding the spirits back home. Kenta's eyes grew tired as the lights faded and eventually shut tight. Whenever I awoke from this dream, I saw Kenta standing in the room with those closed eyes, his clothes dripping with water and then, in as little time as it takes to blink, he would be gone.

"Daddy, can you take me to McDonalds?" Seira shouts as she slips her shoes off and puts on her pink Hello-Kitty house slippers. I can hear Ayano telling Seira to ask again nicely as I come to the front door.

"She hasn't had breakfast yet," Ayano explains. She avoids my eyes and stares at the black gloves tucked into the pocket of my rubber, work apron. Seira runs through the house and searches for Chibi, the family Pomeranian that had to remain with me due to my father-in-law's allergies.

"What about you? Have you eaten?"

"I'll just get something on the way back. I'm not very hungry." She wipes away tiny, yellow crystals from the corners of her sunken eyes. "Be careful tonight," she says. She steps forward as if to embrace me but stops and lays a hand on my chest. She looks up at my face with a softness that has hardened since Kenta's death and then leaves.

When I told Ayano I would honor Kenta's memory by finishing what he set out to do, she didn't understand it. I had stopped working for months, spending time in the garden she had left behind, seeing what had inspired Kenta to mimic the colors of the Earth in the heavens. I tried not to blame myself for what happened. I felt him out there every day, but his presence was always strongest in the workshop where it was cold and blue even in summer. Ayano said I wanted to complete the fire flower for my own fame. She said I disrespected his memory every day I worked. But what Ayano didn't know was that my hands were merely tools, and it was Kenta who was guiding them like some supernatural puppet master, pulling on invisible strings.

Inside, I can hear Chibi barking. Seira has forgotten about her search and lies sprawled out in front of the television like pink flower petals. She's watching a nature program, where children on a boat are carrying a special stereo with wires sticking into the river beneath, telling them whenever an electric eel is nearby through bursts of static. I go to Kenta's room and open the door to let Chibi out, the frigid air enveloping my face like a pair of hands.

At McDonalds, I ask Seira if her mother has been eating to which she answers never.

"Mommy is always yellow," she says, playing with the pink Barbie car that came with her kid's meal. The weeks after Kenta's death, Ayano refused to eat more than the occasional rice ball. Her already slender features had diminished so much that her jaundiced body almost seemed to phase in and out of human sight, becoming a disjointed array of translucent flesh and heat not unlike creatures of the deep sea.

When that first New Year's Eve came, I knew it would be difficult for Ayano. The fire flowers exploding outside, the sounds of children playing with sparklers and morning glories tormented her. I watched her in her room, at her parent's house, while my in-laws took Seira outside to play. Her legs and arms jerked and went into fits of spasms with each blast like little deaths. She'd shake her head violently and curl into a fetal ball. The room became cold and blue in these moments. Ayano pulled the covers over her yellow body as she fell back to sleep. The air grew damp and it became difficult to breathe, as if the room were slowly filling with water one molecule at a time. And at the moment I thought I wouldn't be able to take another breath, Ayano jumped from her bed and ran out from the room, barely noticing my presence. She howled and screamed into the streets with such force and uttering such nonsense that crowds gathered around her. In minutes, the police were called. She ran toward Seira who held a sparkler and grabbed it out of her hand, burning herself. Ayano shrieked in pain. Seira began crying and hid her face in her grandfather's shirt, and I ran to Ayano who did not know what happened, holding out her burned hands like a deity.

"What's wrong with mommy?" Seira asked that night while I was tucking her in.

"Nothing," I said. "She's just very tired." Out in the hall, as I closed Seira's door, I looked down at my fingers, stained with the iodine I used when dressing Ayano's wounds.

Seira is waving to me from the merry-go-round in the McDonald's play area outside as other children spin her around and leap on, the colors of their clothing and blinking shoes becoming a rainbow blur. In a few hours, I will launch Kenta's chrysanthemum. Ayano has promised to be there, but I can't help thinking that she won't show up. The morning after the sparkler incident, she told me about her dreams. She told me how she saw Kenta in the water and how he told her that he had lost his way from the orange lanterns the day he died.

"We all have a color," Ayano explained, "It's part of us, it surrounds us." She said the colors connected us to the world. Most of us are connected to the heavens—the yellows, oranges and pinks, but some to the earth and oceans—the blues, browns and shades of gray. She said Kenta was alone in the darkness, and he saw her light. She said she could guide him back to the lanterns.

Back in the workshop, I can feel Kenta with me. My whole body is cold, almost as if he has stepped into me, moving as I move or perhaps it is the other way around. My in-laws have taken Seira to the beach to pick out a good spot for the show as the festival technicians set up the launch site. Every move I make is accompanied by a memory flashing through my mind as if Kenta is picking out scenes from my life for me to remember, as I load the shells onto trays and carry them to my truck—the day he was born, the first time I let him help me with a launch, the morning before his death when I told him how proud I was of him.

During the slow, careful drive to the bay, the truck seems to move in its own world, wrapped in a bubble on the highway with its own idea of space and time. I feel the past, present and the future rolling into each other—I am a child and man all at once, a new father and a man grieving the loss of his dead son. On the seat next to me, Kenta appears as a child, asking for a story.

"Tell me a story," he says and so I do. I tell him his favorite.

Once, before people, the Earth sprouted giant plants from its heart, rising from the oceans, their giant leaves and red flowers resting on the waves above. Creatures a lot like us but not us lived on the tops of these leaves. They harvested the plants to build towers and bridges and to trade with other worlds that ate the plants. They harvested until the red flowers stopped erupting tiny stars into the sky that would fall back into the ocean and give birth to new plants.

"But then the stranger came," Kenta interrupted.

"Yes, the stranger came," I said. "The stranger collected all the remaining flowers and rolled them into a single leaf and shot them into the sky. As it burned in the atmosphere, millions of tiny red stars showered down on the sea and new plants were born."

Kenta smiles but is no longer a child and then he is gone.

On the launch barge, I place the shells in the mortars including Kenta's chrysanthemum and take my small inflatable back to the control panel on shore. There are thousands camped around the bay—children, lovers, families and their dogs, but Ayano is not among them. One of the technicians hands me the control panel, and I feel as if another bubble is wrapping around me. But this time Seira is with me. I'm at the bay, but I'm also with Ayano at her bedside. My hand is about to detonate the first fire flowers but is also holding my wife's hand. I can hear cheering and applause on the bay and Ayano's words in an otherwise silent room, "It's okay," she says in a voice that tells me her next words may be her last, "I'll be with Kenta, but we'll be together too, all around you."

Then, with my hands, in both times and places, I squeezed Ayano's fingers and pushed the button to launch Kenta's chrysanthemum. The sky above the bay exploded into a deep blue, spanning the horizon, raining down a multitude of stars. As her breathing stopped, the air around Ayano filled with blue water, and a ball of yellow light rose from her mouth, mixing with the blue stars and water, creating a green mist, filling the room until it seeped into the floorboards and into the soil and up past the roof and into the sky, leaving us yet remaining with us everywhere.

Acknowledgments

First and foremost I need to thank my family for being there to support me even if you may not have always understood my path, even when I veered off any kind of path.

To all the editors who gave these stories homes, particularly Bradford Morrow, Kelly Luce, Howard Junker, Jensen Beach, Joanna Luloff, Wayne Miller, Richard Peabody, John Joseph Adams, Andrew Ervin, Thomas Ross, Kate Bernheimer, Joel Hans, Shelby Goddard, Sessily Watt, Em Haymans, and Carmen Gimenez Smith. An additional thanks to Eric Fan for use of his lovely and surreal art.

To the MFA program at Southern Illinois University especially Pinckney Benedict, Beth Lordan, Scott Blackwood, Allison Joseph, Jon Tribble, and Judy Jordan. And to Jessica Easto, Dan Paul, Andy Harnish, Peter Lucas, Jonathan Travelstead, Ashley Sigmon, Mary-Kate Flannery, and everyone else who helped my words and made Carbondale home.

And to Skip Horack for words of early encouragement and to Michael Czyzniejewski whose support and guidance helped me on my path to graduate school and beyond.

A heartfelt thank you to all of my *Zoetrope* friends who, perhaps more than any other group of people, helped me find my literary wings. In particular, I'd like to thank Bonnie Zobell, Mary Akers, Bernice Fisher, Ovo Adagha, Lucinda Nelson Dhavan, Shabnam

Nadiya, Molara Wood, Elaine Chiew, Vanessa Gebbie, Jennifer Lee-
ney Adrian, and Barbara Milton. I'm missing a lot of people here
but know that this book wouldn't exist if it weren't for your support
and wisdom.

And to Cole Bucciaglia for believing in me, for being the most
amazing woman a guy could ask for, for being a shrewd editorial
partner/boss, and for joining me on whatever adventures life throws
our way.

Cole Bucciaglia

Originally from Hawaii and the San Francisco Bay Area, Sequoia Nagamatsu was educated at Grinnell College and Southern Illinois University. He is the managing editor of *Psychopomp Magazine*, and his work has appeared in publications such as *Conjunctions*, *ZYZZYVA*, *The Bellevue Literary Review*, *Tin House's Open Bar*, *The Fairy Tale Review*, and *Black Warrior Review* among others. He resides in Boise with his fiancee where he teaches at The College of Idaho, and will be joining the faculty of St. Olaf College in Minnesota in the Fall of 2016. More info at sequoianagamatsu.net